Alex

Kate Petty is the author of many books for children – pop-up books and non-fiction as well as stories. She lives in London with her husband, they have a son and a daughter.

The Girls Like You Series

Sophie

Hannah

Maddy

Charlotte

Holly

Alex

Josie

Zoe

Dolphin Paperbacks

To Rachel and her friends for all their help.

First published in Great Britain in 2000
as a Dolphin paperback
by Orion Children's Books
a division of the Orion Publishing Group Ltd
Orion House
5 Upper St Martin's Lane
London WC2H 9EA

A catalogue record for this book is
available from the British Library

Typeset at The Spartan Press Ltd,
Lymington, Hants
Printed in Great Britain by
Clays Ltd, St Ives plc

ISBN 1 85881 802 8

One

God, I hate boys! This morning's little episode is typical of life in a house full of brothers.

'Get your great butt out of there, Al!'

'Yeah. Come on, Al. Bet you're reading in there?'

I am, as it happens. I'm reading *Have You Started Yet?* by Ruth Thomson. Leaving it in the loo is as close as Mum gets to telling me important girly things. And why isn't she here now, protecting me from my annoying twelve-year-old brothers? Can't a girl even go to the loo in peace? I know that if I stay in here long enough they'll start fighting each other in a mild sort of way and forget about me.

Needless to say, I *haven't* started yet, though all my friends did, ages ago. But I've had these funny tummy-aches lately, and I've got a ferocious spot bleeping away like a Belisha beacon on my nose, which makes me think it might be about to happen at last. All when I'm about to play in a tennis tournament of course, and wearing lovely virginal white from dawn till dusk. Probably won't. God missed me out when he doled out the feminine attributes, I think. I beg your pardon? Boobs? Surely not. Hips? Straight up and down far more economical. Means you can wear your brothers' hand-me-downs for a start. Oh, and even the name – Alex. No one need even *know* you're a girl.

I'm number three in a family of five. Phil and Joel, seventeen and nearly sixteen. Then me, a girl. Parents thought, oh how nice, let's try for another girl. And what do they get? Double whammy – twin boys. Jack and Sam. Such a blessing. Apparently Mum sank into a deep depression after that and never really came out of it. No, really. She's very depressed, my mum, and fat with it. We don't get on. Dad's great, but Mum? Give me a break. I do try sometimes. But she's no use at all.

I waited for the boys to go away before I emerged from the loo. It was my turn to go to Tescos with Dad. I wanted to stock up on emergency supplies, just in case, but somehow I didn't feel I could involve him. When the coast was clear – i.e., when three of my brothers were squabbling over TV channels – I rang Zoe, my friend and salvation. 'Zo – I need a friend. You going over to Holly's tonight?'

'Of course,' said Zoe. 'Aren't you?'

'No, I'd prefer to relax indoors in the company of my charming family. Of course I am! I've got to go to Tescos with my dad first, though.'

'Mmm. That's exciting. So why do you need a friend?'

'Zoe?'

'What is it Al? What's with the long pauses?'

'Er—'

'WHAT?'

'I think something might be happening that has not been happening before – period-wise.'

'You *think*?'

'Well. I don't know.'

'Listen, you'd sure as heck know if something *had* happened.'

'You mean, it might look as if I'd sat on something?'

'Yeah. Like a squirrel. And killed it.'

'Hey! It's me that makes the jokes! Remember?'

'I'm not joking.'

'Well, OK. It's just that I've had these weird stomach pains, and I'm fearing the worst, since I'm just about to spend a week wearing white.'

'That would be typical. You probably are about to start then. Hey, Al! Welcome to the world of womanhood. Of having a good excuse for being off games and blaming PMT for being grumpy.'

'You wouldn't come shopping with us and pretend the stuff's for you, would you?'

'Sorry, can't do it. Got to see Granny – White Granny – before I'm allowed out for the evening. But I'll bring a nice little selection along with me tonight if you like. How's that?'

'You're a star. Thanks. See you at Holly's then.'

'See you at Holly's.'

I could have asked Holly or Josie rather than Zoe – especially Holly, as she lives closer and her mum's a nurse, after all. But Holly just wouldn't understand me not wanting to ask my own mum – she gets on so well with hers. Actually, Zoe and her mum get along fine too. It's just that Zoe's more sympathetic. She knows a lot about life's little ups and downs.

Holly, Josie and I go back a long way – we were all at junior school together. Zoe came on the scene more recently. I first met her through the twins. Her younger brother Tarquin (yes, Tarquin) is one of their best mates. Believe me, to break in on the twins' little world you have to be quite a personality. And Tarquin is certainly that. So's Zoe. It was great knowing her the day we all started at our comprehensive school. Holly and Josie are both normal looking – you know, medium height, hair tied back, the right clothes. Whereas I was this great beanpole with short sandy hair. Dressed like a boy. Wanted to be a boy at that point – it made life so much easier in our household. And there was Zoe. Tall as me, and dark (her dad's English and her mum's black American). I almost had a crush on her at first. Not really, it was just that she was an exotic new girl and I felt proud that I knew her already. And she laughed at all my jokes. The others do, too. But they take them for granted. Zoe laughed at everything afresh. It did my ego a lot of good.

Holly was having a sleepover. She wouldn't quite tell us why. But that was cool – I'm always happy to meet up with the other three. Especially since I haven't seen that much of them this summer holiday. Zoe's been in Italy. Holly went away for what seemed like weeks to *Barbados* – lucky thing (with her Dad's posh school cricket team). And Josie was off on some music course.

I'm not sure what I've been doing, apart from watching telly and reading a bit. And going up to the Club. The Club is our tennis club, and even calling it a club is a bit of a joke. It's hidden away behind the allotments, with only three courts and not many more members. It's kind of scruffy as well as small – *exclusive* is how we think of ourselves. Seriously, we always have one junior player in the local county finals, if not more. Dad's on the committee. Mum was too, apparently (though I can't believe it), and with five of us kids playing, the Dunbars are core members. I go up most nights. There's always someone I know there (even if it's only a brother). I see more of my tennis friends than my schoolfriends in the summer holidays.

Back to the sleepover. Dad and I unloaded the shopping. I left my brothers to put it away and ran up the road to Holly's (having sneaked out with a few cans of shandy Dad had bought me). It was so late I didn't have time to change out of my sweats from playing earlier – not that any of them would hold it against me. I like going to Holly's house: she and her little sister never seem to quarrel and there's always loads of food on offer – two major points of difference from mine. Holly's mum always shows an interest too, and that's another difference.

So there we were: Zoe, Holly, me and Josie. Josie's a bit silly sometimes, but basically she's OK. She's just had a brace fitted – it's really uncomfortable, apparently. Certainly makes her speak strangely. Holly made us wait until we'd watched *Titanic* and eaten pizzas before she told us the reason she'd gathered us all together. We'd made up beds in their living room, and we were preparing to talk into the night the way we always do – usually about boys if the others have their way, though as you can imagine, boys aren't my favourite topic of conversation. I have enough of them at home.

This was Holly's plan. It was very bizarre actually. She'd met some girl in Barbados who knows someone Josie knows, and four of them who are friends had made this sort of pact at the beginning of the summer holidays to have holiday romances and then report back on them at the end of the holidays. 'And I thought we could do the same,' said Holly. 'It would be brilliant. What do you think?'

'Why?' was my first question. I didn't see the point, personally, especially as Holly's already met some rich guy in Barbados and now she's off to stay with him at his country estate.

The others thought it was a cool idea. Josie's going to Cornwall and she seems to think she might find romance, brace and all. Zoe's not even going anywhere, though she'll be checking out a local Community Theatre Project, so she said she'd try her best to have a romance too. I tried telling them that romance wasn't quite my thing, but when Holly's enthusiastic about something it's infectious and I didn't want to let her down. I'm just playing in a tennis tournament, Mapledon, like I do every year, but I said – yes, OK, I'd try my best too.

Romance, eh? Some girls in our class seem to do and know it all, but that doesn't include us. Posh boy is Holly's first real relationship so now she's hugely keen on 'lurve' and can't stop talking about it. Josie's just as bad. She goes to a girls' school (her parents took her away from our comprehensive after the first year) which seems to make her more interested in boys than ever, but I suspect she's all talk and no action. Zoe is the opposite. She doesn't talk at all, but she could have any boy she wanted. As for me, I'm a 'late developer'. Perhaps, if I am about to enter the 'world of womanhood', Zoe will talk a bit more. I need someone to, because I wouldn't know where to begin, not from a practical point of view anyway. Just fourteen and never been kissed! I am actually the baby of the group – so I do have some excuse. Zoe's nearly fifteen but I only had my fourteenth birthday earlier this month.

Zoe chose a moment when Holly and Josie were in the kitchen to thrust a carrier bag at me. 'How are you doing?' she asked.

'Nothing yet,' I said.

'Well, here's your very own supply of goodies, just in case.'

'Thanks Zo. Wow! I can't believe you lot all know what to do with these things. I'm not sure that I want to learn. Life's nice and simple at the moment.'

'No choice, darling.'

'I just can't bear the thought of growing up like my mum.'

'Grow up like your dad, then. You look more like him.'

'Dads don't have babies.'

'They probably will before long. Then you can find this cute guy to have your babies for you while you get on with all the fun things in life.'

'That would make sense. I'm sure it was having babies that made Mum fat and depressed.'

'Lighten up, Al. It's not like you to get all gloomy!'

'See? Aaagh! I'm turning into her already!'

Two

When I got home next morning it was nearly lunch time. I whizzed straight upstairs and shoved the wretched things Zoe had given me into a drawer. There was a loud knock on my bedroom door.

'Alexandra! What sort of time do you call this? I don't suppose it occurred to you to let us know when you were coming home, did it?'

My mum. Usually I know she's approaching by the slip-slopping of her slippers or the wheezing as she comes up the stairs, but I was obviously too busy rustling plastic bags to hear her. What she said was typical, by the way. She always picks on me. But I was stung, because I'd told Dad last night exactly what time I expected to be home this morning. 'I told Dad. It's not my fault if he doesn't tell you.'

'Oh well. I'm not surprised. Nobody tells me anything. I'm just expected to run around after you all, provide the meals . . .'

(Yawn.) 'Yeah, yeah.'

'Don't talk to me like that, Alexandra.' She always says this, without much conviction.

'Calm down, Mum. I did actually do the shopping with Dad last night. It's Phil's turn to help with the lunch, isn't it? Did anyone ring while I was away?'

'Yes. Several people.'

'Who?'

'I don't know, I really don't have the time to be your

social secretary.' (She always says this, too. In fact, one of the boys usually gets to a phone first in our rabbit warren of a house.)

'Is Phil in?'

'I expect so.'

I dodged round her and knocked on the door of (oldest brother) Phil's room. He was watching Saturday morning kids' TV. 'Philip! Grow up!'

He punched out at me lazily. 'Grow up yourself, kid.'

'Not a kid. Anyway, it smells like a tart's boudoir in here. These *laboratoires* don't need to test their products on animals – they've got you.' I picked up the offending tester bottle. 'Mmm. "Tester". Short for testosterone. Are you practising for the lovely Lana, tonight?'

'None of your business. And since when you have been interested in toiletries anyway?'

'Toiletries! Phil, what sort of a word is *toiletries*? You *are* practising for Lana.'

'You're annoying. Go away. What did you want?'

'Well, I knew that you would have been inches away from the phone from the moment you woke up – so I wondered if anyone had rung for me.'

'Yes.'

'Well, who?'

'What's it worth?'

'Now who's being annoying?'

'Lucy. And Paddy. And Richard.'

'And? What did they say?'

He smirked at me.

'Oh, all right. What do you want me to do?'

'Help Mum with lunch?'

'That's not fair! I did the shopping with Dad last night.'

'That's a *nice* job.'

'OK, OK! Just be prepared for me to extract favours from you, too, in exchange for messages.'

'Lucy – ring her. Paddy – ring him. Richard – do you know where Lucy is? Now go and help Mum. Get her off my case. She's been whingeing on at me all morning.'

'Your methods stink. And so do you!' I slammed the door on his laughter. Actually, Phil is OK. He calls me his 'favourite brother' (ha ha), but he is definitely *my* favourite brother. The twins have always been the bane of my life and Joel, the nearly-sixteen-year-old one, is good-looking apparently (despite the bleached hair), brilliant at everything and a bighead. I sometimes wonder if we share the same parents. Mum certainly treats him differently from the rest of us – she lets him get away with murder. It's particularly harsh because although we're nearly two years apart – his birthday's in October and mine's in August – we're only a year apart at school.

I told Mum I'd help with lunch, though I don't know why she bothers at weekends. We'd all much rather grab a sandwich. Then I phoned Lucy.

Lucy is my tennis partner. My life at the Club is quite separate from my life at school. I'm no one special at school but everyone knows me at the Club. Chiefly because I'm a Dunbar, and it's hard to miss us, even if we are known collectively as 'the Dunbar boys'. As for my Club friends, there are four girls (including me) and four boys in my particular 'crowd': Lucy and me and two girls called Rosie and Harriet; then Paddy and Richard, Neil and Raj (pair of clowns). We've all been taken there by our parents since we were babies.

'Lucy, hi. Has Richard phoned you?'

'Yes, he ran me to ground. He's trying to arrange a practice match tomorrow evening for you, me, Paddy and him.'

'Does it have to be that formal? Can't we just go and knock up like we usually do?'

'He says he wants to practise specifically for the mixed doubles. But I think he really wants a sneak match *against* Paddy, rather than always playing *with* him.'

'That's really stupid. They can knock up any time, like us.'

'Oh, I don't know what his tactics are, Al. I'm not a mind-reader. I just said I'd check with you. Do you think Paddy might object or something?'

'I just don't want to *assume* that Paddy's my mixed doubles partner this year.'

'Why on earth not? He has been for the last three years.'

'I know that. It's just that he hasn't actually mentioned it. I'm worried that he might prefer a *girly*-girl this year.'

'What are you talking about? Why *should* he mention it? He probably assumes you'll be partners like you always are. You *won* the under-14s at Mapledon the year before last – why'd he want to spoil a good thing?'

'Last year we did uselessly.'

'That's because you had to play in the under-16s with him. And because you had to play against *Joel*.'

She was right. And I didn't want her to start on the subject of Joel or I'd never get off the phone. (All the girls, without exception, fancy Joel. They just don't realise what a pig he is.)

'OK. I've got to call him back anyway. I'll ask him about tomorrow night. I'm on for it.'

As Lucy pointed out, Paddy and I have been partners for ages. We play tennis and I make him laugh. But he's been behaving slightly differently this year, and I don't know what it means. He's older than I am so it could be that he's beginning to find me tiresome. People do sometimes tell me to 'grow up'. Anyway, I daren't take our mixed doubles partnership for granted, whatever Lucy says.

'Paddy – you rang.'

'Yes, but it doesn't matter now.'

'What was it?'

'You are – playing – next week, aren't you? Mapledon?'

'Yes, of course. You know I am.'

'Just checking.'

'Duh-uh. *You* are, aren't you?'

'Yes.'

Honestly. He's as bad as my brothers. (The difference is, Paddy and I like each other.) 'Fancy a knock tomorrow night with Richard and Lucy? That's if you're not off snowboarding in Timbuctoo.'

He didn't rise to it. 'Yup. OK.'

'See you about seven? Lucy reckons the adults will be off the courts by then.'

Mum was noisily plonking things on the table, making the point that I'd been on the phone instead of helping her. Slip-slop, plonk – a pile of plates. Slip-slop, plonk – a jug of water. Slip-slop, plonk – the breadboard. 'It's OK, Mum. I'm here now.'

'You're here *now*,' she grumbled. 'But if we all had to wait for *you*, lunch would never happen.' She carried on in this vein, but I blanked her out. The others rolled in: Dad from the local library, where he likes to spend Saturday morning; Phil from watching telly; Joel barely awake and in his dressing-gown; and Jack and Sam, together as always, fighting as always. You can see why I get fed up when Mum picks on *me*.

Dad is the complete opposite to Mum. They're from different planets. I can't imagine how they ever got down to producing the five of us (a ghastly thought – oh well, at least they only had to do it *four* times). Dad works in engineering design and he loves his work. I know he's popular there because I've been to his office and met his work-mates. He plays tennis every Sunday – come rain, come shine – and he coached all of us himself. He's a great stalwart of the club, too, organising tournaments and barbecues and quiz-nights to raise funds. His latest little money-spinner is our Tennis Club Diary. He designed it himself with a handy tennis hint on every page and lots of spaces to fill in things about the matches you're playing. It's a bit naff, but typical of his enthusiasm and I try to fill mine in every day just to please him (which is daft really, because I'd die if he read it). I adore my dad and he always sticks up for me, which kind of compensates for Mum. He treats me like one of the boys in other ways, which is great. He allows me the same freedom and has the same high expectations of me. When it comes to going out to work he'll want me to smash through every glass ceiling there is, unlike Mum, who fell at the first post. Pardon my mixed metaphors.

I hung around long enough after lunch to make sure Jack and Sam were doing the clearing away and then went up to my room. I needed to get to grips with this period business. I was becoming obsessed with the idea now that I might start during the week of the tennis tournament. Zoe warned me that the curse operates on sod's law, so that I was almost bound to start when it was least convenient.

I sorted out my whites. White socks. White tops. White baggy shorts. And a *navy-blue tracksuit*, of course. Pray for cooler weather and I need never take it off! There was my answer. I checked out my white underwear, including my 32A bra (wretched thing, I only wear it because school blouses and tennis gear are so see-through), and lugged the whole lot downstairs to the washing machine. Jack and Sam were still in the kitchen and couldn't pass over an opportunity to comment on my more intimate garments. 'Why do you bother with a bra, Al?' (Jack).

'*I* might as well wear one!' (Sam). He snatched it before I could stop him and paraded round the kitchen, holding it in front of his chest and pointing his fingers into it, Madonna-style. God, I *hate* them! They are *so* gross.

I finally got it off him, and my days-of-the-week knickers off Jack, and stuffed them into the washing machine. Mum came slip-slopping in when it was all over, the twins looking as if butter wouldn't melt in their mouths, and told me to let them get on with the clearing up please. Give me strength.

Saturday afternoon and evening stretched ahead of me, with nothing on the horizon until Sunday evening, so I was glad to be called away from sorting out my tournament gear to speak to Rosie on the phone. (Quick reminder – Rosie and Harriet are the other doubles pair from the Club.) Harriet's away until tomorrow, so Rosie was at a loose end, which suited me fine.

'Make me laugh, Alex,' she said. 'I'm all sad and lonely because I met this boy on holiday and he's still out there and I miss him.'

'Oh not you, too! All these holiday romances are making me sick. Didn't you have anything better to do?'

'Well, we did swim, and er . . . play table tennis, and—'

'Where have you been, exactly?'

'Camping in France. He lives quite near here, though. Says he'll come and watch me play next week – when he gets back. I'm ever so rusty. You don't fancy coming up to the Club later on, do you?'

'Don't mind. Just let me wait for my wash to finish so I can hang it out.'

'Doesn't your mum do that sort of thing for you?'

'Easier to do it myself. She's got five men to look after!'

'That's not the attitude.'

'Try telling her that.'

Joel came up to the Club with me – a mixed blessing. Rosie had eyes only for him at first. And she looked tanned and beautiful, so Joel deigned to speak to her, while I stood twiddling my thumbs. When she finally turned to me, Rosie said, 'Hey, Alex, you look different!'

Joel gave a derisive laugh and went into the pavilion to check the noticeboards. 'What do you mean?' I asked.

'Not sure. Has your hair grown or something?'

'I don't know. Perhaps the daily Baby Bio treatment is starting to take effect.'

'Oh Alex! You're so funny.' (It's easy to make some people laugh.)

Four men were just leaving one of the courts, so we went over to bag it. One of the 'men' was Paddy! I saw that another was his father.

'Hi Paddy!' Rosie and I both said.

'Hi girls,' said Paddy.

'Why didn't you say on the phone that you were coming up today?' I asked him. I didn't like Paddy going mysterious on me.

'Last minute thing,' he said. 'Dad needed someone to make up a four. How are you, Rosie? You're looking bronzed and beautiful.'

'I've just come back from France,' she said.

'She's all aglow because she's in LURVE,' I said, paranoid that Paddy might be on the lookout for a more glamorous partner.

'Is that what happens to people?' he said. 'They get radioactive?'

'Well, girls glow, but boys *sweat*, don't they?'

'Stop it, you two,' said Rosie. 'Go home, Paddy. Let me have Alex. See you on Monday?'

'You *are* playing in the tournament, aren't you Paddy?' I asked innocently.

'Of course he is,' said Rosie impatiently.

'Well, if Rosie says I am, then I guess I must be,' said

Paddy, setting off after his father. 'See you tomorrow, Al!'

I reckon that point went to him.

SATURDAY

Winning is a state of mind. So is losing.

EVENT/S	VENUE	WEATHER CONDITIONS	PHYSICAL HEALTH
Practice	Club	Fine	Rubbish

OPPONENT
Lucy on court, but Paddy really, because he's being odd.

TACTICS
Make him realise he's being odd.

EQUIPMENT
Sarcasm, humour.

COMMENTS
Wish he'd just say straight out that he wants us to be partners as usual.

TOMORROW'S MATCH
Practice: Me and Paddy v Lucy and Richard.

I went up to the Club for our practice as planned on Sunday evening. Joel and Phil came too. Harriet was home from holiday and she and Rosie were sitting round chatting with Richard and Lucy. The arrival of my brothers instantly distracted the girls, so Richard came over to me. I haven't seen him for a while. When he and Paddy first played doubles together they looked hilarious because Richard was a tiny black boy and Paddy was a huge white boy by comparison. Now Richard has just about overtaken Paddy in height. He's extremely good-looking, deadly serious about his tennis and gets very angry with himself when he makes mistakes. He's a good partner though, and he never gets cross with Lucy or Paddy.

'Hi Alex! How you doing, man? You look different. Is it your hair or something?'

'No, Rich. Same old Al. Still look like a boy, only funnier. Where's that Paddy? Shall we go and start? – or we'll never drag Lucy away from my horrible brothers.'

Richard and I went on to the lower court. I was facing the entrance to the Club so I saw Paddy arriving on his bike. He nodded apologetically to us as he got off and then went to detach Lucy from the group around Phil and Joel. Watching Paddy talking to the girls I started to panic all over again. What if he didn't want me as his partner any more? Why hadn't he asked me? I could see the girls flirting with him. It came so naturally to them. Lucy was still at it as they came on court. I hoped she wasn't going to bring up the subject of partners. 'Come on you two,' I shouted, before she had a chance. 'Or we won't finish before dark.'

'Yes, we will,' said Paddy, joining me. 'We'll wipe the floor with them in no time.'

'You wish,' said Richard. 'I'm spinning now and we'll start in five minutes flat. Rough or smooth?'

'Rough!' called Paddy.

'Rough it is!' said Richard, and we were off.

Though I say it myself, Paddy and I make a pretty good team. We just seem to anticipate each other's moves and know precisely when to take or leave a shot. Pit us against Richard getting cross with himself and Lucy being apologetic and we're almost bound to win.

I know Paddy and Lucy so well, it's hard to be objective, but I'll try and describe them. They're both nice looking. Lucy has frizzy dark hair which she ties back. She's got a pretty face with wide brown eyes and a friendly expression. She's shorter than I am (most girls are). Paddy is about the same height as me at the moment, though I expect he'll be several inches taller soon. He's quite stockily built – not long and lean like a lot of tennis players. His hair is light brown, a bit darker than mine maybe, but while I've got bog-standard grey-blue eyes, Paddy's absolute best feature is his dark blue eyes and long, sweeping eyelashes. (We tease him about them. Lucy says they make him look like a giraffe!) He doesn't look that different from when he was a little boy, just bigger. He cycles everywhere and does weights, so he's very fit physically, fitter than the rest of us. Richard's had coaching for most of his life, but Paddy's had very little. Like me, he was taught by his dad, so he's fast but not as stylish as, say, Joel and Phil, who've had loads of professional coaching on top of Dad's.

Paddy was right. We won. It was dusk by the time we finished though, so we went and sat in the pavilion where Rosie and Harriet were still trying to chat up my brothers. Phil considers himself way older than my friends, and Joel's so superior, they weren't getting very far.

We got drinks out of the machine and sat down with them. To my horror, Lucy turned to Paddy and said straight out, 'So, Paddy. You and Al are on good form. I take it you are going to be partners next week?'

Paddy flushed. I was waiting with baited breath for his answer when Joel butted in. 'I want to get back, Phil. You coming? And you'd better come too, Alex, unless you want to walk home alone in the dark. See ya, Richard, Paddy. And you girls. Good luck in the tournament. I'm playing in the Prestige Gold Cup next weekend so I can't do Mapledon this year. Bad form to make the final and then have to drop out.'

Snooty so-and-so. The Prestige Gold Cup is exactly how it sounds. Only extremely talented players need apply, so Joel likes to drop it into the conversation. I gathered up my stuff and trailed home after my brothers. It was the eve of the Mapledon tournament and I still couldn't be certain whether or not I had a mixed doubles partner. Wretched boys. Life would be so much easier if I simply was one.

SUNDAY

Anticipation is more than half the game.

EVENT/S	VENUE	WEATHER CONDITIONS	PHYSICAL HEALTH
Practice	Club	Grey	Still crap

OPPONENT

All my brothers except Phil. Why can't they leave me alone? I feel embarrassed enough without them making it worse all the time.

Mum. Because she never tells them off.

Lucy and Richard really.

TACTICS

Ignore brothers.

Wait for Richard to get cross with himself.

EQUIPMENT

None necessary.

COMMENTS

Hate boys. Hate having to think about periods.

Still don't know if Paddy wants to be my partner in tournament.

Tennis OK.

TOMORROW'S MATCH

Help! Don't know. Only singles and girls' doubles though.

Mixed won't start until Wednesday.

Three

Monday morning. First day of the tournament. Players go in at about eleven, but most matches don't get under way until the afternoon. You've probably watched Wimbledon, so you know how a tournament works, but I always have to remind Zoe and the others. There's boys' singles and girls' singles: under-16 and under-18 are the only important ones. Likewise, boys' doubles and girls' doubles. Mixed doubles starts later on because there are fewer entries, especially in the younger age groups, when you get some real comedy pairings.

The tournament is held at Mapledon, a big club that's about five miles away. Dad drives us if he can get off work. Mum, incidentally, doesn't drive – she must be the only ever 'tennis mum' in history not to do so. More often we get lifts from friends and partners. Lucy usually takes me. Dad took us today because it was the first day and he wanted to check out the draw for Phil and maybe watch a few players in action so he could advise him. The twins played together last year in the under 12s but this year they'd be in the under 14s, and Dad also reckons it would be better if they didn't play together, so they're not here this year, which is great.

So, first things first. Woke up, rushed to loo. No sign of anything, certainly no dead squirrels. Packed emergency supplies into sponge bag, wore dark tracksuit and hoped for the best.

Twins being obnoxious at breakfast because the

attention was on Phil and me. Dad chirpy because he wasn't at work. Mum sighing copiously over the amount of laundry that she was shoving into the machine. She'd already made packed lunches for the three of us. I know I should be grateful, but there's a snack bar at Mapledon where all my friends buy toasted sandwiches and crisps and drinks, and I'd much rather have the money than dull old sandwiches and fruit.

We picked up Phil's partner, Kieron (he doesn't belong to our club), on the way. Nobody said much, we were all feeling too nervous. My stomach was so full of butterflies I began to think that had been the problem all along.

As soon as we rolled into the car park at Mapledon it all came flooding back. Loads of big cars. Keen, suntanned parents dressed in sports gear and sunglasses, exchanging holiday news. An alarming number of extremely small players, all apparently shorter than the tennis racquets they're carrying. Older players quickly finding their own space, where they lounge about as if they own the place. Or that's how it seems. The same feeling that I stick out like a sore thumb, belonging neither with the tinies nor the older ones, and never seeing anyone of my own age.

Then Lucy came roaring up and said, 'Have you seen the draw?' which of course we hadn't because we'd only just arrived, and she kind of skipped alongside us trying to remember it and scaring me silly, thinking I'd been drawn against the top seed in the first round.

The clubhouse was a hive of activity and competitiveness, with parents and players gathered round the flipcharts where the draws were displayed. Comments were quickly relayed in loud voices and even on mobile phones. Phil went off on his own and Lucy dragged Dad and me to the under-16s girls' singles board.

There's nothing random about the draw. It's calculated to ensure that the two best players entered get to play against each other in the final. A huge crowd was gathered there and I had to claw my way through to the front. Miss A. Dunbar. Every year I scan the list for Alexandra or Alex, but at Mapledon it's all very formal and old-fashioned. Here I'm Miss A. Dunbar, just like Wimbledon. Where is she, this Miss A. Dunbar? Hey! Dad called out from the back at the same time as I saw it. I was seeded! It looked as though I was expected to make it to the quarter-final. I looked more closely. My first match was against someone I'd never heard of – a Miss P. Chang. I ducked out of the crowd. 'Well done, Alex,' said Dad. 'That's excellent when you must be one of the youngest.'

Lucy had checked the doubles draw already, so I didn't need to fight my way over to that one. She wanted us to bag a practice court together. Dad said he'd go and sniff out the competition. There was no sign of anyone else from the Club, so I followed Lucy out on to one of the back courts. It was fortunately quite a bright, chilly, windy day. I reckoned I would be able to stay in my tracksuit all the time if I was lucky.

We giggled our way through a few stretching exercises. Meanwhile, the first and second seeds from the under-16s – Connie and Alicia – incredibly talented black cousins, came and starting knocking up on the court next door. They had all the professional gear, and wasted no time chatting (unlike us). 'We might have to play them,' Lucy whispered when we met at the net, 'if we get to the semi-finals.'

'As if!' I whispered back. 'I think I heard that they're both sixteen next month. Junior Wimbledon and stuff. We wouldn't stand a chance.'

'Probably won't get that far, anyway,' said Lucy. We hadn't played for long when I caught my name coming over the tannoy. 'Would Miss A. Dunbar and Miss P. Chang please go to Court Six. First Round, Under-16 Girls' Singles. Miss A. Dunbar and Miss P. Chang.'

Paddy came rushing over. He seemed almost as nervous as I was. 'Did you hear that, Alex?'

'Yeah, yeah,' I said, trying to sound casual as I put my tracksuit top on back to front. 'Miss *Pchang*, here I come. Sounds like a ball pinging off a racquet doesn't it?'

'Will you stay and knock up with me, Paddy,' asked Lucy, 'or are you going to watch Alex?'

'I'll knock up for a bit,' he said. 'And then we'll go and support Al. I've got a feeling old Pchang is quite good.'

'Funny how Alex's nicknames always stick, isn't it?' said Lucy.

Pchang and I reported in to the desk and then solemnly made our way to Court Six, followed in procession by both her parents and her coach. Dad came over to hug me and wish me good luck and said he might come over later. Pchang was a very silent girl. We knocked up and chose ends, and almost all she said was 'Sorry' from time to time. She wasn't bad at all – but I was better. The constant encouragement from her parents and coach began to get on my nerves which was good because it gave me an edge. I won the first set 6–4 but I was actually losing the second when my troops arrived: Lucy, Paddy, Dad, Phil and Kieron. Every time the Changs shouted encouragement, my lot shouted counter-encouragement. (In fact I could sometimes hear Paddy muttering 'pchang!' when she hit the ball really hard.) It was what I needed. I equalised and then went on to win the match. Pchang and I – her name was actually Philippa, I discovered (Phchang!) – shook hands and went off with our separate bands of supporters. I felt quite sorry for her. She didn't seem to have any friends at the tournament at all.

As we walked back to the desk, Kieron said to me, 'Hi, I'm Kieron.'

'I know,' I said. 'Kieron, you travelled here in the car with me this morning. And we've met tons of times before, dipstick!'

'Oy!' said big brother Phil. 'That's no way to speak to my partner!'

'Sorry,' said Kieron. 'But you were sitting in front, and I was a bundle of nerves. You must look different this year. Anyway, well done. Philippa was expected to win that.'

'Oh. Does that mean I wasn't seeded after all?'

'Think we might have got it wrong,' said Dad. 'But never mind – you'll get to the quarter final, you see. You show 'em!' That's my dad, always expecting the best of me.

I gave our score to the desk and was told that the doubles were starting later in the afternoon, which gave me several hours off. Lucy had a bye (no match) for the first round which meant she was also free until our doubles match. We found somewhere to sit and eat our sandwiches (her mum makes them too).

'How about Kieron talking to you then!' she said after a gulp of Tango.

I had some too. I burped before replying. 'He obviously mistook me for someone who would be flattered.'

'Well, he is rather gorgeous. Old Phchang quite lost her concentration when he and Phil turned up.'

'Are you trying to say that's why I won the match?'

'No, no! Not at all. I was just going to say that maybe you *should* be flattered by Kieron taking an interest.'

'Watch my lips, Lucy.' I burped again. 'Boys do not interest me. OK? I am surrounded by them. I wouldn't mind *being* one. Though on second thoughts, they're all so disgusting that I'm glad I'm not.' Lucy gave me a disapproving look as if to remind me that burping was pretty disgusting, so I did it again, just to irritate her. 'Anyway, what's the hurry all of a sudden?'

'Dunno,' said Lucy. 'It's just that once you do start fancying boys, you can't help it, I suppose. And it's a laugh,' she added.

'Yeah,' I said. 'Like going to the dentist is a laugh.'

'You're a hopeless case,' said Lucy. 'Let's go and mingle, maybe watch the boys. I heard Paddy being called a few minutes ago.' I followed her without another word because suddenly – far more terrifying than any tennis match – the challenge of the 'holiday romance' reared its ugly head. I thought of telling Lucy about it, but she'd only jeer at me after that last conversation. How on earth was I going to carry it off? Kieron had been a bit interested in me, hadn't he? I couldn't think of anyone else. But no. It was impossible. It's just not the sort of thing I do. Where would I even begin? How could I have agreed to anything so utterly ridiculous?

We made our way over to the clubhouse. The whole place was heaving now. All the old hands were there. Another family large enough to rival us Dunbars are the Smarts. Tom and Louise Smart are the same ages as Joel and me. There are at least two younger ones and an older one. I've always found Louise annoying – she wiggles her bottom when she walks, making the pleats of her tennis skirt swing from side to side. Anyway, they have a big house with a swimming pool, close by in Mapledon, where the cliquey set get invited to barbecues. Joel's been, naturally. I don't think Phil's ever quite made it into the in-crowd – or the 'Smart set' as everyone calls it – but Kieron probably has.

'Uh-oh,' I whispered to Lucy. I'd just spotted Ethlie (known as Deathly Ethlie by all and sundry), a sad girl I wanted to avoid. She's one of those people who latches on and pretends you're her friend. We had to put up with her last year. Sounds mean, I know, but she follows us around like a little dog and laughs uproariously at absolutely everything I do, whether it's meant to be funny or not. I could say, 'I've got a hideous incurable disease and my grandmother's just been run over by a bus,' and she'd titter and say, 'Oh no! Really? Ooh, you are funny, Alex!' Lucy and I immediately ducked out of sight like naughty six-year-olds.

We wandered out to the main courts in search of Paddy's match. The singles were in full swing now, and almost every court was occupied. We spotted Richard in the distance, so we followed him and ended up in the right place. The game had just begun. Paddy's opponent was listed as R. Laxton. Richard sat on the bank with another boy, presumably a friend of R. Laxton's. We joined them. 'How's it going?' I whispered to Richard. I didn't want to distract Paddy.

'Nothing yet,' whispered Richard back.

'He and Robin seem to be pretty evenly matched,' whispered the friend. 'Hi, I'm Charlie.'

Charlie and Robin. They were new to me. They were similarly-built, lanky boys, Charlie dark, Robin fair. I was about to carry on the whispered conversation, but I saw Paddy glaring at us, so I gave him a wave and shut up. It was a close match. Robin had style and Paddy had speed. It was probably going to depend on who was fittest – and in that department I'd put my money on Paddy any day. At 5–all Robin spent a lot of time picking up tennis balls and retying his laces while Paddy waited calmly for him to carry on. Charlie started talking again when they were changing ends at 5–6. 'Robin's my partner,' he said, 'so I want him to win, but the other chap's got a lot of power hasn't he? This could take a while.'

I was about to say, 'And Paddy's my partner,' but I didn't dare tempt fate. 'Paddy's from my club,' I said, 'so I want *him* to win. Is this your first year here?'

'We don't normally do this tournament,' Charlie said. 'In fact we're doing the Cup this weekend, too, so I seriously hope neither of us gets into the finals!'

'Is that the Prestige Gold Cup? That's a bit bad, isn't it?' I asked. 'One of my brothers has dropped out of Mapledon because he's playing in the Cup. Why doesn't Robin just let Paddy win now, if that's the case? Paddy's desperate to get to the final.'

'Don't blame us,' said Charlie. 'Our coach tells Robin and me what to do.'

'Is he called Batman?' I asked. 'Tennisbatman?' It was a pathetic joke, but Charlie guffawed loudly, making Paddy fluff a serve.

'Do you mind if I take that again?' Paddy asked Robin, frowning in our direction.

'Sorreee,' I mouthed, and then Lucy was tugging at my sleeve because our names had been called for the first round of the girls' doubles and we had to check in.

'I don't know,' she said. 'It's so unfair. Guys chatting you up all over the place, and you couldn't care less. That Charlie bloke obviously thought you were really funny.'

The thought popped into my mind that Charlie might *just* be another candidate in the romance stakes, but it popped out again very quickly indeed. My brain finds that sort of data difficult to process.

'I try my best to amuse. I want to go to the locker room first, Lucy. Will you check in for us? I'll be there in a minute.' I ran off, praying that it was too much fizzy drink making me desperate for the loo.

'You OK?' asked Lucy when I found her.

'I'm fine,' I said. I was, thank goodness. We were drawn against two very blobby girls who were far, far worse players than we were. And of course that meant that Lucy and I played atrociously. Our audience consisted solely of Ethlie. We scraped through the first set and we were 4–all in the second set when Dad turned up to watch, closely followed by a triumphant looking Paddy. Lucy and I were doing badly, returning stupid donkey-drops with even stupider donkey-drops that went in the net. We'd reached the point of snarling at one another. Dad and Paddy called me over as I was walking back to serve. 'Play *hard,*' said Dad. 'Bend your knees.'

'Run in to the net, Al,' said Paddy. 'Go for the kill! By the way, I won.' I gave him a thumbs up sign as I moved back to the baseline.

'Come on, Alex!' came another voice as I was about to serve. Charlie and Robin had stopped to watch. I served an ace and we went on to win 6–4 without dropping a single point.

'I could murder an iced bun,' said Lucy, after we'd all shaken hands and come off the court.

'So could I,' said Robin, surprisingly.

'I thought I'd go and watch Phil,' said Dad.

'I'll come with you,' said Paddy. 'He should win, shouldn't he? Are you coming too – er—?'

'Charlie,' said Charlie. 'I'm the partner of the guy you just thrashed, Robin. Is the Phil we're off to watch Phil Dunbar?'

'My brother, yes,' I said, following them and guiltily leaving Lucy to the mercy of Robin. She didn't look that unhappy about it.

'Wow,' said Charlie. 'So you're Joel Dunbar's sister, too, presumably?'

'Might be,' I said.

Charlie looked taken aback and then laughed. 'You get used to her,' said Paddy appreciatively. 'How do you know Joel, Charlie? He's not playing this week because he's in the Prestige Gold Cup at the weekend.'

'Everyone knows Joel, don't they?' said Charlie,

warming to Paddy, though I don't know if Paddy was warming to him. I was glad Charlie glossed over the fact that he was in the Cup too. Paddy wouldn't have approved.

I linked my arm in Dad's and let the two boys walk ahead. Charlie was a very suave guy with thick, shiny brown hair and long tanned legs. Beside him Paddy looked stockier than ever. 'How's my girl?' said Dad. 'Glad you picked up at the end of your match. It would've been terrible to have lost to those two.'

'Shocking, wasn't it? I'm glad you all arrived and shook us out of our apathy.'

'Quite a little entourage you're building up. Who is this Charlie boy?'

'I dunno. Someone who knows Joel. I haven't seen him play, but Paddy managed to beat his partner, Robin.'

'Good old Paddy. It would be super if he won this year.'

Phil was playing on one of the main courts and there was quite a crowd watching him. As Dad and I tried to slide inconspicuously into the row of seats, people turned round to smile at us. Charlie, who ended up sitting next to me, was impressed. 'The Dunbars are obviously good people to know!' he said to Paddy.

Lucy and Robin turned up soon after, closely followed by Ethlie. Ethlie schmoozed up to Paddy while Lucy grimaced at me behind their backs. Brother Phil was winning easily, so Lucy and I climbed over the seats and went to the clubhouse to look at tomorrow's draw. 'Ooh, thank goodness we've got rid of Deathly Ethlie! She doesn't half give me the creeps.'

'Me too,' I said. 'Still, Paddy's got her now.'

'Paddy's always nice to everyone,' said Lucy. 'Which means that Ethlie will love him for ever, like a faithful dog.'

'Arf, arf,' I said, and we both giggled.

The first day's play had gone more or less according to plan, if you didn't count the little upset I'd created by beating Phchang. Tomorrow I'd be playing against one of the Blobs, and Lucy was up against Rosie, which was a bit tough on both of them – it's rotten playing against a friend in a tournament.

I was ready to go home. I suddenly wanted my own room and a break from all these people. My stomach was feeling odd again. Lucy rang her mum on her mobile and she offered to give me a lift home. I went to tell Dad just as everyone was clapping Phil for winning. Louise Smart had gathered a little group around her that included Kieron and the new boys, Charlie and Robin. Ethlie was hanging in there, no doubt hoping for a Smart invitation, but Paddy was on his own, not to be drawn.

Lucy nudged me. 'Ask him,' she said. 'Go on, ask Paddy about the mixed doubles now.'

'I can't, Lucy,' I said. 'He's in unapproachable mode. You see? That's what I mean when I say he's acting strangely this year. He never used to be like this.'

'Shall I ask Richard to ask him?' she said.

'No, that's daft. Right now I just want to hope for the best.'

My room is my haven. There is possibly only one decent

rule in our house – which you might even have noticed – and that is that all of us knock on each other's bedroom doors, including the twins (who have separate rooms). It doesn't mean to say that someone won't knock and come crashing in straight away, but they will knock. After supper I lay on my bed to think. I put on my *Little Mermaid* CD and gazed up at the ceiling. All right, I know my taste in music is immature and it wasn't a hundred percent appropriate to my mood, but never mind.

I always feel like this when I've been with a large group of people. I find myself wondering where I fit in with them and whether they like me or not. Louise Smart usually ignores me, so that's nothing new. Ethlie's a pain. I don't *want* her to like me. But Charlie and Robin – the new guys – had been friendly. I smiled at the memory of Kieron introducing himself to me. Kieron who's been Phil's partner for ages. Idiot! Something has definitely changed this year. Perhaps it's me! All those people saying I *look* different. I don't really *feel* different. *I* don't think . . .

I stood up and went over to my mirror. To be honest, I don't look in it very often. It's not as if I wear make-up or anything. It's true, my hair, which always goes fairer in the summer, is a bit longer. My fringe has grown so much, I have to hold it back off my face with a hairband or clips. And it's just about long enough at the back to scrape into a silly little ponytail. You can see I've got eyebrows and cheekbones now! Maybe that's why people think I look different. I pulled my teeshirt into a bunch at my back and regarded myself closely. Perhaps I do go *in* a bit more at the waist than I did before (I certainly don't go *out*, up top). Perhaps Alex Dunbar is a girl whether she wants to be one or not. That could be a plus in the holiday romance allure and seduction stakes. Help! What have I let myself in for here? Two boys being friendly is a zillion miles away from actually 'having a romance'.

My big gorilla poster grinned knowingly down at me from the wall. Time *he* went.

MONDAY

A good tennis player is like a good orchestral musician: rhythm, timing, pitch and harmony are all crucial to the performance.

EVENT/S	VENUE	WEATHER CONDITIONS	PHYSICAL HEALTH
U-16 singles U-16 doubles	Mapledon	Bright but chilly	Unpredictable

OPPONENT
Phchang (singles).
The Blobs (doubles).

TACTICS
Didn't mess about (after bad beginning).

RESULT
Won both matches.

EQUIPMENT
Dark tracksuit proving useful.

COMMENTS
Good to see people again. Kieron introduced himself to me! Two new guys, Charlie and Robin – v. friendly. Ch thinks Joel's cool so he must be a bit of a prat. STILL not certain about mixed doubles. This is getting silly, but for some reason Paddy makes me nervous when we're not playing.

TOMORROW'S MATCH
One of the Blobs for singles. Two unknowns for doubles. Should be an easy day.
Lucy has to play Rosie (poor both of them).
Paddy has to play Richard (also poor both of them).

Four

Tuesday. Day Two. Mum was in a particularly filthy mood this morning, even though Dad had left for work and the twins had gone off somewhere (Joel was still in bed) so only Phil and I were having breakfast. I wondered if the tournament had something to do with it. Too many packed lunches perhaps. We weren't needed at Mapledon until midday, so it wasn't even that early. She wearily offered us a cooked breakfast, which neither of us wanted, and huffed and puffed as she made our sandwiches.

'You all right, Mum?' asked Phil cautiously.

'Why shouldn't I be?' she asked, somewhat ungraciously, I thought. Phil and I both shut up and refrained from saying, 'Because you're sighing even more than usual', and got up from the table to put our things in the dishwasher.

'Kieron's offered us both a lift today,' Phil said, once we'd made ourselves scarce.

'That's OK, Lucy's picking me up any minute now,' I said.

'Kieron seems unaccountably interested in you – did you notice?' Phil asked.

'Was "unaccountably" his expression, or yours?'

'I don't understand you, Alex. Most girls would be really chuffed.'

'Well, I'm not most girls, am I? I'm your favourite brother, remember?'

'Maybe it's time you started being my favourite sister.'

'Your *only* sister.'

'Shut up. You know what I mean.' He punched me on the shoulder.

Lucy and I went straight to the clubhouse. I felt as if we'd been coming to Mapledon for weeks already. There were fewer parents today. There is a certain type of professional tennis mum who attends these tournaments. She is always tanned, always wears sunglasses and usually has a mobile phone. There is another sort – floral and harassed, usually with millions of small boys – but she is quieter and less in evidence than the first sort. Mrs Smart – 'call-me-Janice' – is one of the first sort, the professional ones. Not only does she organise her own brood very efficiently, she likes to have a handle on all the other 'young people' as well, at least the suitable ones, e.g. Joel.

Louise annoying-bottom-wiggle Smart and her mother were surrounded by quite a few players. They were talking about the possibility of a swim that evening and a big barbecue towards the end of the week. It was a toss-up between the Thursday and the Friday. Louise plumped for the Thursday because more people would still be left in the tournament. So it was put about that the Smarts were having a barbecue party on Thursday evening. It was the sort of general invitation that carries its own subtle rules – the sort that I assume excludes me. The so-called 'Smart set' know who they are.

After checking the board, Lucy and I walked over to the outer courts. Nice coolish day. Nothing odd about keeping tracksuit bottoms on, certainly not at the level of tennis I'd be playing. We polished off our sandwiches and then ambled on court for a knock-up and a gossip. Lucy finds me very frustrating, I know.

'I really – like Kieron – don't you?' she said between strokes.

'He's all right,' I said. 'Bit of a bighead.' I wasn't ready to tell Lucy about the romance project – not yet anyway.

'What about – Charlie?' she said.

'He's a – prat,' I said, whacking the ball for emphasis. I wanted this conversation to end.

'I thought you liked him. Anyway, he's not a prat,' she said. 'He's – fit.'

'That doesn't stop him being a prat. He's a fit prat, but he's only interested in me because I'm Joel's sister.'

'You're lucky. I wish I had a brother to make people interested in me.'

'You really don't wish you had brothers,' I said. 'Anyway, I want people to be interested in me for myself, not because of some pain of a brother.'

We were interrupted by Phil and Kieron. 'I hope you're not talking about me,' said Phil. 'Thought we'd come and knock up with you, give you a run for your money.'

'Blimey,' I said. 'To what do we owe this honour?'

'Well, it certainly wasn't my idea,' said Phil, herding me down the other end with Lucy, 'but I'm sure it will improve your tennis.'

I love playing against the boys. It raises my game like anything. I had some great baseline rallies with Kieron.

'She's practically as good as you!' said Kieron to Phil.

'Rubbish!' said Phil, hitting a hard, spinning shot onto my backhand.

I wasn't having that. I went up to the net and started

sending volleys at him, fancy ones, leaping and turning ones. I beat him nearly every time. Then, when my back was turned he childishly whacked a ball straight at me. It hit me on the arm.

'Ouch!'

'Should have volleyed that one, shouldn't you!'

'Phil!' The pain had brought tears to my eyes. 'You hurt me!' Honestly, boys just can't help being competitive. Even Phil can't cope if I win occasionally.

'Hey, are you all right?' Kieron was all concern.

'Course she's all right,' said Phil gruffly, possibly feeling just a teensy bit foolish.

'There's a great red mark!' said Kieron. 'Charming brother you've got!' He smiled sympathetically at me. I caught Lucy at the edge of my vision looking all wide-eyed.

Announcements were coming over the tannoy. We stopped to listen. 'Better go, Kieron,' said Phil. 'Sorry, Al. Didn't mean to hurt you,' he said. And punched my arm – just where he'd hit it with the tennis ball.

'Ow!'

'Oops. We'll be off then,' said Phil. 'Really didn't do *that* on purpose, Al.'

'See ya!' said Kieron.

Lucy came over to inspect my wound. 'Wow. That must have been worth a bit of pain, just for Kieron's sympathy! Did Phil hit the ball at you on purpose, then?'

'Oh yes,' I replied. 'Like I said – brothers! Boys! Who needs 'em?'

'Well, at least he didn't *punch* you on purpose.'

'No. But why are you so protective all of a sudden?'

'I just didn't believe someone as nice as Phil could be such a bully.'

'You ain't seen nothin', then. That *is* nice compared to Joel and the twins, who have horribleness down to a fine art.'

I had to go off to an outer court with my opponent, one of the Blobs from yesterday. Blob Two was our only audience. I remembered Dad's words from the doubles, and ruthlessly set out to win every shot. Which I did, more or less. Blob One spent a lot of time drinking water and wiping her brow when we changed ends, and Blob Two spun out the business of moving the little tabs that show the score, but I still won 6–0, 6–0 in little more than half an hour. Humiliating for her, but not a lot I could do about it. We shook hands and wandered off to report. Lucy appeared almost immediately because we had a doubles match to play. 'Lucky I'm not too exhausted,' I said. 'Do I get time for a drink?'

'Yes, of course,' said Lucy. 'But they know it's practically a walkover. These two are even worse than the Blobs. It'd better be a walkover because I've got my match against Rosie later this afternoon, worse luck.'

'Yeah, that's a tough one.'

As predicted, the doubles was a piece of cake. We didn't give them a chance. Lucy faltered momentarily when she saw Robin and Charlie stop to watch for a few minutes, but the whole thing lasted about the same time as my singles match.

'Not a bad way to warm up, I suppose,' said Lucy as we came off. We went ahead to report, and our opponents followed. It was still early.

'How soon do you think you could play your singles against Rosie?' the woman on the desk asked Lucy.

'Straight away if I can just grab a bottle of water and go to the loo first. Wish me luck, Al. Glad I haven't had too much time to think about it.'

'Break a leg,' I said as she disappeared into the clubhouse.

Ethlie materialised beside me. She always comes too close and invades your personal space. 'How did you do?' she asked me excitedly.

'I won,' I said. 'And then we won.'

'Oh no! Really?' (*Why* does she always say that?) 'Who's your partner for the mixed doubles?' she asked, when our score had been logged in. 'No one's asked me – I don't seem to be very popular with the boys, but there are so many to choose from this year.'

'Dunno,' I said nonchalantly, wishing she'd spontaneously combust. I didn't want to admit, even to myself, that I belonged in the same partnerless category as Deathly Ethlie.

'D'you think one of the new guys – Charlie or Robin – might play with me?'

A horrible image of two sleek tigers tossing a scrawny little terrier between them filled my mind, but I refrained from communicating it. 'Dunno,' I said again. I could see her ears pointing, I tell you. 'Ask them and see.'

'Oh no! Really?' she tittered. 'Anyway, I'd much rather watch the girls. Shall we see how Rosie and Lucy are doing?' she asked, as if the pair of us had a jolly action-packed afternoon all mapped out.

Damn. That's where I was heading anyway, and I

didn't want Ethlie doing her limpet act. 'Must just go to the loo,' I said in an effort to lose her. 'You go on.'

'I wouldn't go off without you!' she said. 'Don't worry, I'll wait.'

Argh! I went to the loo anyway. I'd got used to the turmoil that was once a well-behaved gut, but I couldn't altogether relax. I eavesdropped on at least two conversations to eke out the time down there. Both were interesting, and both kept me locked in the loo until the speakers had gone away. The Blobs were discussing my earlier singles match. Blob One was saying, 'I really should have won. She wasn't supposed to get beyond the first round.'

'It was a shame you were having a bad day,' Blob Two said supportively. 'I'm sure you would have beaten her hollow on a good day.'

'You wish,' I said to myself as the door closed behind them. But then I heard Louise Smart's distinctive cut-glass voice.

'Guard the door for me, will you?' she said to whoever it was. She carried on from inside the cubicle. 'You are coming tonight, aren't you, Claire?' (I don't know Claire, but I pictured the girl with smooth dark hair I'd seen with Louise earlier.) 'You must see this Joel Dunbar guy, he's gorgeous. It means I'm going to have to ask Phil and the sister, so he simply can't get out of it, but he's worth it.'

'Isn't he here this week then?'

'No. He's in the Cup this weekend.'

'With Chris Green and co?'

'That's the one. We'll have to go over there and watch them,' said Louise, flushing the loo and emerging. I couldn't hear much after that against the sound of the cistern. Didn't need to really, did I? So, I was about to receive a Smart invitation. Lucky old me. Maybe I should say no, and persuade Joel not to go either. Nah. Wouldn't work. I came out. Oh God – there was Ethlie.

'Thought you'd died,' she said cheerfully. (I wish *you* had, I thought.) But then I was saved by the tannoy. Ethlie was called to play a doubles match and I was able to go and watch Lucy without her.

Lucy and Rosie had gathered quite a crowd. I looked on from a distance for a while to gauge how it was going. Lucy, who was serving well, seemed to have the edge on Rosie right now. I decided to stay back until the end of her service game. Wouldn't do to distract my friend and make her do a double fault. When she won the game I moved closer to hear the score. It was 7–6 to Lucy and still the first set.

My friends from the Club were sitting right at the front. I don't think I would have liked that if I'd been playing another Club member, but they were being very quiet and unobtrusive. I sat on the bank behind with Charlie and Robin. We were out of the players' line of vision there. 'Hi guys!' We spoke in whispers.

'How did you get on?' asked Charlie.

'Six–love, six–love against the Blob. Same against the Ugly Sisters. What about you?'

'Haven't played yet,' said Charlie. 'I think I'm against that guy over there – if he's R. Vishindi. Is he good?'

'Terrible,' I said.

'Really?'

'Course not. He's probably a bit better than Neil there and not quite as good as Richard, who's playing Paddy on Court Three – depending which side of bed he got out of.'

'Temperamental then?'

'Hey, these are my guys! I'm not giving away secrets!'

'What d'you mean, your guys? Are you going out with *all* of them?'

'Don't be daft. They're from my club, that's all.'

'The Miss A. Dunbar fan club? Can I join?'

I giggled.

'Ssh, you two,' said Robin. 'They're playing a tie-break.'

I looked over and saw Lucy glaring at me as she picked up some balls from the corner of the court. I shut up.

Lucy won the tie-break and they launched into a second gruelling set. You don't want to lose when you play a friend, but you don't quite want to win either! Robin, Charlie and I moved back even further, so we could carry on chatting without disturbing the players. Robin's mobile went off at one point, so it was a good thing we did.

'Robin's girlfriend,' said Charlie. 'Jealous. Won't leave him alone. Switch it *off*, Rob! You're distracting everyone now.'

Robin smiled. He was a good-natured bloke. 'Better than having to listen to you two chat each other up all day.'

Charlie and I both protested. 'She's funny,' said Charlie. 'I can't help it if she makes me laugh.'

'We can go and watch Paddy playing Richard if you want,' I said. 'Then you can imagine Raj being somewhere in between, and see for yourself. I usually try and watch Paddy anyway.'

'Is Paddy your boyfriend then?' asked Charlie.

'NO!' I said – too loudly. Rosie glanced over crossly this time. Charlie and I got up to go. Robin gestured that he was staying. 'I have boy *friends*, not a boyfriend! I'm just one of the lads, me.'

We wove our way across to where Paddy and Richard were slugging it out. Paddy waved at me, but he eyed Charlie suspiciously. I don't think he knows what to make of him.

At that moment it started to rain. Players all over carried on for a minute or so, but then the heavens opened and everyone rushed round the courts gathering their racquets and tennis balls before joining the mad dash for the clubhouse.

It was like an overcrowded party with everyone crammed in there in their damp tracksuits. I found myself washed up against Phil and Kieron and Louise Smart mid-conversation. 'Good,' said Kieron. 'So that means Alex will be coming.'

Louise looked embarrassed. 'Oh, of course,' she said.

'What?' I asked. 'What am I coming to?'

'For a swim at my house this evening,' said Louise. 'Presumably you and Phil and Joel can all come together?'

'Shouldn't count on Joel doing anything,' I said.

'Oh surely you and Phil can persuade him? Can't you?' Louise was pleading.

'We'll do our best,' said Phil. 'I'd like to come.'

'The weather will need to be a bit better before I go swimming,' I said, wanting her to beg.

'Don't feel you *have* to come—' Louise started to say.

I was enjoying this, not that swimming was actually

my recreation of choice at this precise moment. 'Oh no, I'd love to come, Louise. Thanks so much for inviting me. Anyway, it looks as though the rain's easing up already.'

I started to move away because I'd spotted Paddy heading in my direction. 'Bloomin' rain,' he said grumpily, when we managed to get close enough to speak. 'I was just getting into my stride against Richard there. Beginning to needle him, go for his soft spots, make him riled with himself.'

'Steady on,' I said.

'–And then we have to come off and be nice to each other.'

'Well, you are partners the rest of the time.'

'Yeah, but I want to *win* this year.'

'I know. Calm down, calm down.'

'Oh go on, just make a joke of it like you do about everything, why don't you.'

'Well I'm sorry,' I said, confused. Paddy's usually so cheery. I'm not used to seeing him frustrated and cross.

'No, I'm sorry,' he said. 'Shouldn't take it out on you.' He raised his head to apologise, the old giraffe-lashes fluttering like mad. Then he looked over my shoulder. 'Charlie-boy's after you again. Excuse me if I go and vent my frustrations on something that doesn't answer back.' He set off, but Charlie waylaid him.

'Hey! Hear you're coming to the swim, Alex. Are you coming too, Paddy?'

'What swim?' asked Paddy.

'At the Smarts',' said Charlie.

'They don't invite people like me,' said Paddy, sounding a bit brusque, and went on his way.

'But they do invite people like you?' said Charlie to me.

'Oh, Lousie only invited me because she wants my brother Joel to come,' I said.

'Lousie? Oh! Ha! I see, *Louise*!' Charlie guffawed.

'Not that I shall encourage him, of course.'

The rain had stopped and people were going outside again. Lucy passed on her way back to her match. Robin was with her. (I think the girlfriend on the mobile is fighting a losing battle.) '*You're* coming to the Smarts' tonight, Rob, aren't you?' said Charlie. 'Alex is.'

Lucy looked incredulous. '*You're* going to the Smarts', Alex?' she said. 'Blimey. You must tell me why, some time. Anyway, must fly. Got a match to win.'

'How's it going?' I asked.

'Fine,' she said. 'But I think I'm better off without you and Charlie being there. Wish me luck!' She went off.

'Louise did mention it to me,' Robin was saying to Charlie. 'But I'm not sure I'll come. I haven't been fishing for an invitation like you have. I don't really know the girl.' He set off after Lucy. 'Told Lucy I'd carry on watching her. You coming?'

'No, we've been banned,' I said.

It was a strange afternoon. I wanted to watch Lucy's game against Rosie, but Lucy had given her orders. Normally I support Paddy, but I knew that if Charlie came along we'd end up laughing and joking and putting him off. So I found myself wandering around the courts with Charlie until my friends' matches were all finished.

I learnt a lot about Charlie. He and Robin are at school

together. Charlie's home set-up sounds pretty similar to the Smarts', though they have a tennis court rather than a swimming pool in the garden. Charlie plays with his dad, like I do. He's got two older sisters who aren't that interested in tennis any more, but it's clear his entire family dotes on him – which might explain the self-confidence. He says they talk about girls all the time at school, but he doesn't know many apart from his sisters.

We almost missed the call for his match against Raj. In fact it was Raj's name I recognised first. 'You'd better come and watch me then,' said Charlie, 'since the others have banned you. And you'd better be supporting me because all your friends will want Raj to win, won't they?'

I went to the clubhouse with Charlie. Paddy and Lucy were there buying drinks for Richard and Rosie and trying to hide their glee, but it was obvious from Richard's and Rosie's faces that they were the losers. Horrible, all round. It didn't seem tactful to stay.

This was the first time I'd seen Charlie play and I was curious. Raj is good – most people find it hard to beat him. But Charlie – Charlie was a top player. Wow. He was in another league. How could he not get to the final? How, if they both made it to the semi-final, could he not beat Paddy? I didn't like to think about it. Sneakily I found myself looking for weaknesses so that I could tell Paddy. But there were none. Charlie's play was flawless.

One-by-one my friends – Raj's friends – came to watch. Lucy arrived with Robin. Some sort of chemistry is definitely at work there. I almost hoped Paddy wouldn't turn up to this match. He wanted to win the championship so much – seeing Charlie would only depress him.

Charlie was making mincemeat of Raj. I wanted to shut my eyes – hide behind the sofa. Charlie served ace after ace. When Raj did manage to return, Charlie slammed the ball onto his weak backhand, scooting up to the net to finish with a flash volley – the few times Raj actually managed to get a rally going. Poor Raj fought back as hard as he could, but Charlie was utterly brilliant. I heard Phil and Kieron behind me. 'That kid shouldn't be in the under-16s, should he?' Kieron asked me.

'He's fifteen,' I whispered back.

'Glad I won't have to play him, then,' said Phil.

'Joel will in the Prestige Gold Cup,' I said.

'What's the kid doing here if he's in the Cup? Not that it's any of our business. Probably best to keep quiet about it. Still. Do Joel good to be brought down a peg or two,' said Phil. He looked at me. 'You OK, Al? Sorry I whacked you earlier. Don't know what came over me. Very juvenile.'

'Some mistake, surely?' I said. 'Can this be a brother apologising?'

'I had a go at him for hitting a girl,' said Kieron.

'I have the dubious privilege in my family of not being treated as a girl,' I said.

'So Phil told me. Weird family.'

Charlie served four aces in a row and won the match. Paddy appeared with Ethlie as we were clapping, though I could see the others from the Club looking more inclined to boo.

'Hello everyone,' said Ethlie brightly, as if we might be glad to see her or something. No one returned her greeting because Charlie was being congratulated by Robin, and Phil and Kieron don't do that sort of thing. It was left to me.

'Oh, hi,' I said, pretending I'd only just noticed her.

'Guess what!' she said, glancing winsomely (oh, hideous sight) back at Paddy.

'They've just posted the mixed doubles list. People are putting their names down.'

'Well, I know who I'd like as a partner,' said Charlie, smiling broadly at me.

'Time to go,' said Phil with the usual Dunbar immaculate timing. 'You might as well come with us, Alex, since we're all going on to the Smarts'. See you, guys!'

Five

Please be there. Please be there. 'Zoe?' Phew.

'Zoe, I've been invited to a swimming party.'

'Lucky old you. What's the problem?'

'Have you forgotten?'

'Oh! Has it finally happened?'

'Well, no, actually.'

'Don't worry then. Not about swimming anyway. Cold water seems to stop things. Hanging around in a swimsuit might be more of a problem.'

'It's not the warmest evening.'

'Exactly. Make your excuses and get dressed I would. Now enough of that, it's yukky. How's the tournament going? How's the *romance*?'

'What romance?'

'Don't tell me you've forgotten already. Blimey, you're the one with a short memory. Holly's idea?'

'Only joking! How could I forget. It's loony expecting me to do this. Not that romance isn't being shoved down my throat every minute—'

'What do you mean?'

'Well, Lucy, my partner, is forever saying, so-and-so fancies you, hadn't you noticed. Then there's this guy called Charlie who thinks all the boys from the Club are my boyfriends.'

'Sounds a riot.'

'It's cool. But do I absolutely have to have a romance? I said I would, didn't I?'

'Pledged.'

'Oh dear. You know I don't have romantic leanings.'

'Well, you'd better start now. Sounds as though you have plenty of choice.'

'Aagh! I dunno, Zo. Anyway, got to go. Phil's hovering. Our lift to the swim is due any minute now. Thanks for the advice! I'll call you again and you can tell me your stuff. Byee!'

Phil was in big brother mode. 'Get your act together, Alex. Kieron should be here by now.'

'Where's Joel? Have a go at him, not me. He wasn't around for supper. Is he even out of bed yet?'

'Good point.' Phil went in search of Joel and I ran up to my room. It wasn't that warm outside – I could wear my jeans and a vesty top. Take a sweatshirt. As for swimming things – well, not much choice really. Same one I had last year. Speedo, bright blue. I bundled it up in a beach towel and shoved it in a Tescos carrier bag with my sweatshirt along with a wrapped ST and a hairbrush.

The doorbell rang. I wanted to bypass Mum, so I ran to open it.

'Are you all ready?' said Kieron. 'You look nice.'

I tried desperately to think of a funny response to the compliment, but none came. 'Er, yes. Thanks. I'll call the others.'

Joel arrived on the scene looking as though he really had just got up, his bleached hair all tousled. He dangled a pair of swimming shorts on his finger. No towel. 'Use yer bag, Al?'

'Get your own.'

He didn't. Phil reappeared smelling of the tester.

'I think Phil has high expectations of this swim, don't you?' said Kieron to me with a smile.

'Oy,' said Phil. 'Leave it out. Just because I'm not a scruff like my little bro.'

The three of us followed Kieron to his mum's car. Kieron sat in the front with her and we three Dunbars bundled into the back. 'Ouch!' said Joel. 'You got a hedgehog in here?'

'Get off my hairbrush, slaphead!'

'Shut up, you two, or Mrs Mallory will think we're always like this,' said Phil, embarrassed.

'Speak for yourself,' I said. But we continued the journey in silence.

'Shall I pick you up at ten-thirty?' said Mrs Mallory as

she disgorged us onto the pavement outside the Smarts' (mock) Tudor mansion.

'OK for you guys?' asked Kieron.

'Fine for me and Al, thanks,' said Phil. 'We're playing tomorrow.'

Joel looked uncertain. 'I'll wait and—'

'—see if you get a better offer,' said Kieron. 'That's not a problem, Joel. Thanks, Mum. See you later.'

The swim was in full swing. It was a decent-sized pool in a little fenced-off area of its own. Joel immediately pulled his T-shirt down at the front, stripped off his bottom half and changed into his swimming shorts right there, to hoots and squeals from Louise and her friend Claire (the girl I'd heard her talking to in the loo). Phil and Kieron nabbed the oldest Smart. 'Hi guys, how's it going?' he said.

'Where do we change?' Phil asked him.

'Go back indoors. Guys in my room. Girls in Louise's.'

'Where's that?' I asked. I didn't like the sound of this.

'Across the landing from mine. You'll see.'

Louise's room was really tidy apart from the piles of clothes where people had changed. One wall was completely covered in posters – and none of them were of gorillas. She had fitted wardrobes, her own basin and a mirror surrounded by film-star lights. Luxurious but quite old-fashioned compared with, say, Holly's or Zoe's, but then I always knew my friends had more style than the Smarts. Just less money! There was no one else around, but I felt self-conscious. What if someone came in when I had nothing on?

I was standing in the middle of the room clutching my carrier bag when the door flew open and Claire and Louise did come in, on gales of hysterical laughter. They were very wet, with sarongs over their bikinis.

'Did you *see* Joel changing?' squealed Louise.

'He doesn't mind what people see, does he?' said Claire.

'That's because he knows they'll be impressed,' said Louise, giggling. And then '–Oops! Sorry Alex. Didn't see you there!'

'Can you tell me where the loo is?' I asked. *I'll get changed in privacy thank you very much.*

'At the end there!' Louise just about managed to point me in the right direction before collapsing into giggles again. I heard her saying, 'Oooooh! That's Joel's sister. Do you think she heard me? What if she tells him?'

Fat chance, I thought, locking the door. He's big-headed enough as it is. It was a tiny loo. I struggled out of my clothes and into my Speedo. No mirror to check how I looked. I wrapped my beach towel round my shoulders and unlocked the door. No one around. The boys must have gone on ahead.

It was kind of scary in the garden. The evening sun was making long shadows on the lawn and there was a lot of drinking and smoking and snogging going on amongst the older ones. I couldn't see anyone I knew well enough to speak to. Remembering what Zoe had said, I wanted to get into the water as quickly as possible, so I went through the gate to the pool, dumped my bag and towel and dived in.

Actually it was gorgeous. The water was just the right

temperature – really refreshing. I surfaced and looked around me. Joel was at the shallow end, holding on to the bar behind him and showing off his six-pack to advantage while the girls played 'splashy splashy' with him. Phil and Kieron were mucking about with an inflatable shark with some much younger kids. As I swam over to join in the shark game, the boys went off to help splash Joel. The little kids were pleased to see me. 'Who are you?' they asked. 'Will you help us get on the shark?'

'I'm Alex,' I said, 'Dunbar.'

'My big sister loves Joel Dunbar,' said one of the little girls, who looked just like all the other Smarts except that she was wearing arm bands and huge swimming goggles.

'She must be mad, then,' I said. 'Come on, who wants to be lifted on to this thing? Shall we see how many we can get on it?'

'She is mad,' said the littlest Smart. 'I think boys are yuk.'

'And so do I,' I said. 'What did you say your name was?'

'I'm Scarlett,' she said. 'Scarlett Sarah Smart. Triple S. My middle name's Sarah in case I get fed up with the Scarlett.'

This was more information than I required, but it was good to talk to at least one Smart who didn't immediately give me an inferiority complex. I climbed onto the shark with difficulty and complete loss of dignity. (Have you ever tried it?) Once I was on I was able to haul Scarlett up in front of me. I leaned back to lift up the other kid, when – Wuh! the shark shot out from between my legs and catapulted us both backwards into the water.

'That was brilliant!' shrieked Scarlett, unfazed.

'I want a go! I want a go!' cried the other kid.

'I didn't do it on purpose, you know,' I said.

'Well, you've just invented a new game then,' said the other kid. 'My turn now.'

So I struggled onto the shark again, lifted up the other kid, leant backwards and – Wuh! out shot the shark again. It was fun playing with these two. Certainly more fun than wimpy splashing games with Joel. We did it quite a few times. My extra weight made the shark shooting out far more spectacular than if it had just been the kids. In the end, 'call-me-Janice' came and hoiked Scarlett and friend out of the water because it was their bedtime. I was quite disappointed. 'And who are you, dear?' she asked, patronisingly.

'Alex Dunbar,' I muttered.

'Oh, Joel's little sister!' she said, standing on the edge of the pool, Scarlett clinging to her leg. 'Joel!' she trilled. 'Joel, your little sister's looking rather cold!' Gee, thanks.

'I don't think he'll be very interested,' I said. 'I'm fine. I'm getting out now, anyway.' I hauled myself out and stood up. *Little* sister indeed. I towered over 'call-me-Janice'. Where was my bag? I needed my towel and clothes. Not only did I feel exposed in my unglamorous swimsuit and goosepimples, I remembered Zoe's advice. I looked around. I was sure I'd left it there, by the hedge.

Then I remembered following Mrs Smart's glance to where Joel sat surrounded by admirers – wrapped in *my* towel. I heard him playing to the gallery. 'Sorry folks – the sex with a shark entertainment has sadly drawn to a close. And – oh, excuse my goosepimple – it's a sister. In fact I think I can spy *two* goosepimples!'

A red haze came down over my eyes. I strode over to him. 'Joel!' I shrieked. 'You BUM! Give me back my towel!' I saw the Tescos bag and then saw that he had tipped everything out of it. Everything.

'Which towel?' said Joel. 'This one—' he held out the beach towel, tantalisingly, 'or this one?' You can guess what he held up then.

Amidst the ensuing laughter I moved exceedingly fast. I smacked him and grabbed my towel almost in one move. While he was still reeling, I snatched up my bag, stuffed everything back and ran to the house, my eyes smarting with tears. Louise and Claire weren't the only ones I'd recognised amongst my mockers. *Charlie* had been chortling too. And I thought he was my friend. Not any more. I never wanted to speak to him again.

I locked myself in the loo again and peeled off my wet swimsuit. It was not a comfortable operation. I dried myself and dressed and then didn't know what to do. I looked at my watch. It was nine-thirty. Could I stay in here for a whole hour?

Obviously not. I heard voices coming up the stairs. I was used to eavesdropping on Louise now. 'That Joel,' she said. 'You have to laugh, don't you? I know he's cruel, but he's just so funny when he gets going.'

'I thought he was a bit mean,' Claire said. 'His poor sister. I would have died.'

'Well—' said Louise, and then they shut the bedroom

door and I was spared the end of her sentence. But then she came out again to go to the loo. She rattled the doorhandle. 'Yoo hoo!' she said. 'Is someone in there? Hurry up, I'm desperate!' So I had no choice but to emerge. Boy, did I want to go home. Without a word to Louise I went downstairs. I found a room with a telly in it, switched it on, and sat in front of it. Most things I can make a joke of (just like Joel, I suppose) but this situation was without comedy as far as I was concerned. I felt utterly, utterly humiliated. The tears started to flow again.

After a while, someone came into the room behind me. It was Kieron. 'Alex?' he said. 'I've been looking for you.'

'Can't think why,' I said.

'Just wanted to see if you were OK. I don't understand why your brothers turn into such pigs around you.'

'Joel's always a pig.'

'Maybe. But Phil's my mate. He's OK.'

'I know. Phil is usually OK. Don't know what got into him this morning.'

'Jealousy I expect.'

'Don't know what he's got to be jealous of.'

'You, of course. He didn't like me paying attention to you.'

'Only this morning he told me to stop acting like a brother and start acting more like a sister. He can't have it both ways.'

'Confused, obviously.'

'Anyway, Kieron. It's all right. I'm used to it.'

'Well, you shouldn't be. What do your parents say when your brothers tease you?'

'Honestly, it's only Joel. The twins are just stupid and Phil's the good guy normally. They wouldn't do it in front of Dad – or Mum. You know what families are like.'

'Well, I've only got one older sister, and I wouldn't *dare* treat her like that!'

I paused. For a brief moment I wanted to tell Kieron about how useless Mum was. How she never stuck up for me, or stopped the boys taunting me. How the sun shone out of Joel's bottom as far as she was concerned – he could do no wrong. But I didn't.

'Kieron? You're a cool guy. Why are you being nice to me?'

'Because, just like in the movies, my friend's kid sister is turning into quite a babe.'

'Oh stop it.'

'There. Made you smile. No, you're OK, Alexandra Dunbar, and don't let anybody tell you otherwise.'

I laughed and played air violin.

'You're your own worst enemy,' he said.

'No. Joel's worser.'

'Worser? No such word! Anyway, it's nearly time to go. Are you coming out to hold your head up in front of those idiots or do you want to lurk in here until my mum comes?'

I didn't know.

'Come on. I'll protect you.'

'OK!' Suddenly the world seemed a better place. Kieron was kind and nice and wanted to make me feel better. Maybe, *maybe* – this was how a romance began. I didn't think so, but what the hell! 'You're on. Kieron, *darling*!' I linked my arm in his.

'Steady on,' he said, and we went out into the garden.

'Kieron! Your mum's here!' someone yelled almost as soon as we'd gone outside and found Phil (who hadn't got lucky on this occasion).

'OK Phil, Alex?' said Kieron. 'Not sure we should give Joel car-space, frankly.'

'What do you mean?' said Phil.

'If you weren't there it's better that you don't know. He was extremely unfunny at your sister's expense.'

'Oh well, that's nothing new,' said Phil. We'd reached the car.

'You come in the front, dear,' Kieron's mum said to me. 'Don't see why you should be squashed in the back with those two.'

Ah. A friend and sympathiser! No wonder Kieron showed a bit of respect.

'What about Joel?' I said.

'What about him?' said Kieron as we all saw him running towards the car. 'Drive on, Mother.'

TUESDAY

Always stay on top of the game whether you are winning or losing. If your opponent drags you down you have not only lost the game but the pleasure of playing.

EVENT/S	VENUE	WEATHER CONDITIONS	PHYSICAL HEALTH
U-16 singles U-16 doubles	Mapledon	Grey and rainy	Unpredictable
Swim at Smarts	Smart Towers	Cleared up	!

OPPONENT
Blob One
Ugly Sisters (doubles)

Joel

TACTICS

Ruthless both times.

None

RESULT

Won both matches.

Humiliation. I definitely lost.

EQUIPMENT

Dark tracksuit still proving useful.

Blue Speedo – inappropriate.

COMMENTS

Tournament OK. Me, Lucy and Paddy both through to next round. Also Charlie and Louise and Tom Smart. And others who I can't remember. Charlie v friendly all day but I've gone off him big time since he was one of the people jeering with Joel. MIXED DOUBLES DILEMMA. What shall I do? Charlie virtually asked me to partner him. (Definitely won't now.) Deathly Ethlie was homing in on Paddy. HELP! Paddy is not his usual self.

PS Kieron is so nice. He'd be perfect for the romance I suppose. But the thought of actually kissing him – kissing anyone properly – is just too scary.

TOMORROW'S MATCH

Singles and mixed doubles (if I have a partner).

Singles v Unknown (her name's Megan Birchill).

Mixed doubles. Partner: Unknown. Opponents: Unknown.

A days of Unknowns for me.

Lucy v Ethlie.

Paddy v First seed (Paul Sisson). Tough one. Paddy can do it!

Joel arrived home about an hour after we did. Mrs Smart had given him a lift herself. I heard him ranting at Phil about being left behind. I heard Mum weighing in too. I heard the phone ringing and Dad saying he was sorry but Alex had gone to bed. I went to sleep feeling OK – but I still had *no* idea what I was going to do about a mixed doubles partner, or a romance.

Six

'Hello?'

'Hi, it's me, Lucy – how was the swim last night? D'you feel like coming to the Club this morning? I want to hear all the gossip.'

'No you don't. But I'll come anyway. I've never set eyes on this Megan Birchill girl I'm playing today, so I need to be prepared.'

'I'm against Ethlie, and there's no way I'm losing to *her*.'

'Arf arf!'

'And the mixed doubles start today. Hey, guess what! Robin rang last night and asked me to be his partner.'

'And what did you say to him?'

'Well, "No", of course. I've got a partner, haven't I?'

'More than I have.' I looked at my watch. Ten o'clock. 'I've got to do a bit of house stuff. See you up there in half an hour.'

I could hear Mum approaching. Slip-slop, sigh. Slip-slop, sigh. 'I suppose I'd better do your sandwiches then,' she said wearily.

I wish she'd just give me money. 'It's OK, Mum, I'll do them. I'll do Phil's as well, if you like.' Anything to get her off my back. I didn't want her to stop me going out.

'Would you, dear?' Mum's round face positively lit up.

'Yeah, fine.'

'Well, well. That's a first.'

'It's not, Mum, and you know it. Precious Joel might not do anything to help, but I bloomin' well do.'

'Poor Joel. He says you all drove off without him after the swim.'

'Only what he deserved. He was vile to me last night.'

'Oh, I'm sure it wasn't on purpose.'

See what I mean?

'His word against mine, Mum, and I know who you'll believe. Now, excuse me. I want to make two packed lunches.'

'I wish you and Joel would get on. I would have loved an older brother when I was your age.'

'Maybe, but *two* older brothers, not to mention two younger brothers, is a wee bit over the top.' I spread the bread and laid cheese slices on.

'Are you sure Philip likes cheese slices?'

'If he doesn't, he should make his own sandwiches.' *Go away, go away*. I was saved by the twins. They burst into the kitchen, squabbling, so Mum had to go and sigh at them for a while. I stuffed the sandwiches into a carrier bag, grabbed a couple of apples and filled a bottle with squash. That would have to do. 'I'm off out for a bit now,' I called, picked up my racquet and made a dash for it.

'I really like Robin.'

'You really liked Kieron yesterday.'

'I know, but that was sort of "from afar."'

'I think Kieron's nice.'

'Excuse me? Would you mind repeating that? Did Alex Dunbar actually say she liked a boy?'

'I like loads of boys. But Kieron was – sort of – well – nice to me last night.' I looked away, remembering. 'Tell me about Robin, I know you're dying to. I also know he has a jealous girlfriend who phones him all the time.'

'Emma.'

'So he's told you about her?'

We made ourselves comfortable on the seat outside the pavilion. 'Yes. He's fed up with her. Said he wanted to get to know new people.'

'Like you.'

'Exactly. He went on about how he'd watched me playing and how our styles would go well together, but I knew that was all bull.'

'Are you going to go out with him?'

'Alex!'

'Well, that's what all this is leading up to, isn't it?'

'I don't know yet. We just had a nice long chat, that's all.'

'I dunno. It all seems like a silly game to me. You like him, he likes you. So why don't you just cut out the middle bit and go out together?'

'Because the middle bit is what's fun. I despair of you sometimes Alex.' She stood up. 'We'd better knock up if we're going to.' We walked on to the court. 'Anyway. I'm quite looking forward to the mixed.'

'Huh. So would I be if I was in it.'

'What do you mean?' Lucy hit a ball to me.

'*I* still don't have a partner, remember?'

'Seems to me that you have a choice of at least two. Three if you count Robin.'

'So who's number two?'

'Didn't Charlie say he wanted to be?'

'Not in quite so many words. Anyway, I'm right off Charlie.'

'Paddy seemed to think Charlie had already asked you.'

'Well he didn't. Did you talk about it with Paddy then?'

'Yes. He seemed a bit down, actually.'

'Can't help that. He should have asked me himself.'

'You're impossible.' Lucy practised a couple of serves on me. 'So what has Charlie done to blot his copybook and how was Kieron "nice"?'

'It's a long story. As I said, you don't want to hear it.'

'Meanie. You know that makes me all the more curious.'

'It's just that at the swim last night Joel went in for a particularly unpleasant form of ritual humiliation of his sister and Charlie found it as amusing as the rest of Joel's cronies.'

'What did Joel do, for goodness sake?'

'Oh, just tipped out my bag and held up its most *intimate* contents for all to see and laugh at. Hilarious really. I was so upset. Which isn't like me, I know. So I went off in a grump and Kieron came and found me and tried to cheer me up.'

'I said he fancied you.'

'Nah. He's far too old. But he said I'd turned into a "babe".' I vaguely hoped that Lucy would pounce on this piece of information as a definite sign that romance would surely follow. I waited for her reaction.

'Wow! I'm jealous. Not that everyone hasn't been

saying the same thing. You know – "I say, the Dunbar girl has *grown* up a lot hasn't she?" nudge, nudge, etc . . .' (No, I wasn't getting any help here.)

'I don't *feel* any different.' I slammed the ball as hard as I could. It landed in the net. 'Who, exactly, has been saying this?'

'Oh I don't know. People.'

'Anyone would think that it was unusual to grow up at our age.'

'Yeah, yeah.' Lucy wore her despairing look again. 'But Paddy and the mixed doubles thing is important. You really don't want him to end up with Deathly Ethlie, do you? Nab him as soon as we get there. Ring him, *before* we get there.' She was right. Forget holiday romance. The partner business *had* to be resolved.

The first people we saw when we arrived at Mapledon that Wednesday morning were Charlie and Robin. I hadn't managed to get hold of Paddy on the phone, though believe me, with Lucy standing over me I had tried. I cut Charlie dead, the toad, and ran off to look for Paddy. Absolutely no time left for misunderstandings now.

I found him – with Ethlie! Maybe it was too late already. 'Paddy, could I have a word?' I asked, finding that I felt really nervous all of a sudden. Paddy actually looked relieved to be rescued.

'Excuse me, Ethlie,' he said. So polite, Paddy, bless him. He turned his back on her. 'What is it, Alex? Is something the matter?'

'It depends.'

'Depends on what?'

'On what you've been talking to Ethlie about.'

'Her options! Her GCSE options, if you must know!'

'Not partnership options?'

'Alex!'

'Be my partner?'

'In the mixed doubles? Well—' He paused, horribly.

'Oh. Never mind. If you've already asked someone – never mind.'

'I haven't, Alex. It's just that—'

'As I said, never mind. Doesn't matter.' I headed off.

'Alex!' Paddy called after me. 'Of course! I'll put our names down, shall I?'

And do you know what? I went back and threw my arms round him.

'Hey! It's no big deal!' he said, going pink.

'Thanks mate,' I said, and punched him on the shoulder.

They were starting to call players for the singles. I wanted to find Lucy again before her match against Ethlie and I wanted to check out the mysterious Megan Birchill.

I found Lucy being wished good luck by Robin, with much twinkling and giggling on her part. Now the mixed doubles was safely sorted I had a sudden brainwave about the romance. I could cheat! It would mean letting Lucy in on it, but never mind. I waited until Robin had moved away. 'Hey, Lucy. Want to do me a favour?'

'What is it this time? Don't tell me you haven't had the guts to ask Paddy. I don't know what's got into you this year.'

'Nothing's got into me. It's him who didn't ask me in

the first place. Anyway, I have and he's said yes. Though he was still a bit iffy.'

'So what's this favour then?'

'Do you want to have a romance for me?'

'*What?*' Loads of us were converging on the desk. It wasn't easy to hold a conversation.

'I'm meant to be having a romance and reporting back to my friends – Zoe and that lot,' I said, as if it was something I did every day. 'It's just that you look as if something might happen with Robin anyway and that would spare me and you could just give me the details and I could pretend it was what happened to me.'

'You're mad, Alex,' said Lucy, raising her voice across the crowds. 'Go and have one of your own, for goodness sake. Right now we've got matches to play. Good luck!'

I vaguely recognised Megan. I'd seen her around, but she looked older than most of the under-16s – big and shambling, with a Janet Street-Porter voice. Her whites were definitely less than white and her trainers were at least last year's. She was even taller and noisier than me! 'Hi Alex, how you doing?' she said when we met.

'How did you know which one I was?' I asked.

'You're a Dunbar aren't you? I've met your brothers.'

'I apologise right now for anything they might have said or done.'

'No need. Joel's the cute one, isn't he? And Phil's the nice one?'

'You could describe them like that I suppose. And I'm the female one.'

She laughed. 'You come here every year, don't you?'

'Well, yes. It's what we do. I don't even think about it.'

'My PE teacher made me come. The council pays for me. Hi Charlie! Hi Robin!' she said. I looked up to see the pair of them. I blanked Charlie again, the treacherous one. 'Do you know those two?' she asked as we walked on.

'Just met them this week,' I said.

'They're cool,' she said. 'Nice to have guys who aren't part of the usual crowd, not to mention the Smart set. Wouldn't say no to an invitation there though. Their house is supposed to be dead posh. Not special friends of yours are they, the Smarts?'

'No,' I said. 'Though I think Charlie would very happily be part of the Smart set. He's already a member of the Joel Dunbar fan club, which makes me think he must be a few sandwiches short of a picnic.'

'He told me he was a member of the Alex Dunbar fan club yesterday. I thought he was a friend of yours.'

'*Was* is the operative word there.' We'd reached our court. 'Let's knock up quickly and get started, shall we? Anyone in the mixed doubles has got at least one more match today.'

'Don't think I want to win this,' said Megan. 'The winner gets to play either Louise Smart or Connie King, don't they?'

'Oy, don't be so negative! In this match you get to play the terrifying Alex Dunbar, who's far better than either Louise or Connie. Allegedly.'

Needless to say, I won. I shouldn't have done because I was playing so badly. I was easily distracted by each and every spectator, especially Charlie and Robin, and Paddy. There were questions I wanted to ask Paddy, and Charlie seemed to want to communicate something to me – he kept doing telephoning gestures. Phil and Kieron appeared, too, Kieron waving and smiling. Even Tom Smart passing by made me lose my concentration. His dark hair had gone all bleached and spiky, like Joel's, overnight. Must have done it at the swim. Fancy wanting to look like Joel!

My brain kept going back to this romance thing and my 'pledge'. I'm always up for a challenge – I don't want to be the wet one of the group.

'Thanks,' Megan was shaking my hand. We'd finished. All our spectators had gone off to play their own matches. 'I really enjoyed that. I didn't expect to get a single game off you. I never thought we'd still be going an hour and a half later! The council don't get any return for their investment, but that's their tough luck. And you get to pay for the drinks!' She rattled on as we headed for the clubhouse. 'Who's your partner in the mixed doubles?'

'Paddy Gardner.'

'Don't think I know him. Do you know mine, Max Freeman? He's only playing in the mixed for a laugh. He's quite good, but not a serious player. Music's his thing. And girls. Excitable, is Max. You'd like him. I'll introduce you.'

I refrained from asking what made her think I was interested in an excitable guy. Partly because, yet again, I was pondering, maybe here was someone I could have a romance with if Kieron didn't work out – now Charlie's so definitely off the list. Aagh! This is so not me!

I bought the drinks and we went over to look at the

draw for the mixed. Paddy and I were up against fellow Club-members Harriet and Neil straight away. Shame. Hey! Charlie was playing with Louise Smart, and they were first seeds. Not surprising – someone must have clocked Charlie's play, and Louise is brilliant (annoyingly). Hmmm. Charlie and Louise, eh? What about the Alex Dunbar fan club? I wasn't jealous. I hate Charlie, don't I?

Get a grip, Alex. I really was all over the place this morning. When Megan left I decided to take my sandwiches and watch Lucy playing Ethlie, though knowing Ethlie she'd think I was there to support *her*. I went over on my own, passing Charlie's match on the way. Robin saw me and joined me. 'You going over to watch Lucy? I'll come with you.'

Lucy has great concentration. She smiled at me and Robin – especially at Robin – but she didn't alter her game. Robin checked his mobile was switched off and sat back with a smug expression on his face. Emma was now an ex-girlfriend it seemed.

'Did you find a partner for the mixed?' I asked him, between games. 'Yes,' he said wistfully. 'Lucy's already got a partner, so I agreed to play with Louise Smart's friend Claire. Louise asked Charlie last night, you see. That's when he called you.'

'Called me? What do you mean?'

'Last night. Quite late. We wanted to be quite sure first that you and Lucy couldn't be our partners. You two were the ones we wanted. But then Lucy told me she already had a partner.'

'Someone did ring last night after I'd gone to bed – I heard my dad telling them. But messages only get passed on at a price in our house. So that was Charlie, was it?' *But I hate Charlie. He laughed at me.*

We shut up. The score was one set all. Ethlie, despite her unattractive personality, is quite a good player. She's left-handed and she's got a very solid backhand. The trick is to get her up to the net and alternate hard shots with lobs – she's not much of a runner. Robin and I agreed that that was a good tactic, and I whispered it to Lucy when they were resting before the final set and Ethlie had her back turned.

The sun came out and it was turning into a beautiful late-summer day. (I didn't want it getting too hot.) Lucy followed our strategy and won the third set easily. When they came off Lucy went dreamily over to Robin. You could practically see the hearts and flowers dancing in the air between them. Blimey. I'd definitely use Lucy's romance if I couldn't concoct one of my own.

'Hello, gorgeous!' I jumped. It was Kieron. He was addressing me. 'And how are we this morning?' He gave me a penetrating look.

'Fine now,' I said. 'Thanks.'

'That's all I wanted to hear,' he said. 'Thought I'd catch you before Phil and I go on. Must dash. See you.'

'Alex? Al?' It was Lucy. 'Excuse me?'

'Sorry, I was miles away.'

'Obviously. I think you're *in* there.'

'Where's Robin?'

'Gone to find Claire, more's the pity. They want to get going on the mixed at three-thirty apparently, but most of the boys' matches seem to be still going on. I suppose they're quite close at this stage, like mine was. Thank goodness Richard's out of it – he won't be too tired. Paddy's got a tough one, hasn't he?'

'Yup. He's playing the first seed. Actually I'd forgotten. He was probably really keyed up this morning.'

'But you're sorted for the mixed now?'

'Yes. But not in other ways, Luce. My brain's all over the place today.'

'Glad I'm not playing with you till tomorrow then. What's the problem?'

'Let's go and sit over there.' There was a white plastic garden table and chairs over by the practice wall. We laid claim to them, discouraging anyone from joining us.

'OK. Out with it.'

'There isn't an "it" really. It's just that I'm still furious with Charlie for ganging up against me last night, and I don't think he's even noticed. Paddy's still acting odd – unfinished sentences and stuff. And Kieron's being dead kind, but I don't quite know what it's all about. I asked him last night – I think he just feels sorry for me.' I let out a sigh. 'And I'm meant to have this romance.'

'You make it sound like an exam or something!'

'I see it's not like that for you and Robin.'

'He's so cute, isn't he? Pity you're off Charlie – we'd have made a good foursome.'

'Stop it, Lucy. I wouldn't have wanted to have a *relationship* with Charlie, even if I did still like him.' (I didn't want her jumping to conclusions.)

'OK. So Charlie's in disgrace and has disqualified himself in the romance stakes. Which leaves Paddy and Kieron. Which one shall it be?'

'*Paddy*? You *are* joking?'

'Don't see why I should be. He's a top bloke is our Paddy. You get on well, know each other's shots, so to speak.'

'Paddy is my *mate.*'

'OK, OK. No need to get all vehement about it. So that leaves Kieron.'

'And Max.'

'You are so full of surprises, Alex Dunbar. "No romance! No romance!" you cry, and then you suddenly come up with an unknown contender. And who is Max?'

'Oh, no one. It's silly. He's Megan's partner – only here for the mixed, and she said we might get on. You can see what a state I'm getting into. Anyone's fair game.'

'Except Robin.'

'OK. Not Robin.'

'Kieron then,' said Lucy.

'OK,' I agreed. I sat up. '*What* did I just say?'

'Romance with Kieron. Go for it.'

Seven

'Hi babe!' The voice came from behind us as we headed for our first mixed doubles match. Paddy looked round sharply. It was Kieron again.

'Hi Kieron,' he said.

'Since when have you been a babe, Paddy Gardner?'

said Kieron. 'I was addressing Miss A. Dunbar here. Good luck both of you, anyway.' He waved his racquets cheerfully as he turned left and we turned right. My knees felt quite weak. How was I ever going to do this romance thing with him?

'Nice guy, Kieron,' said Paddy. He'd just beaten the first seed to a place in the semi-final and was in a magnanimous mood.

I wanted to change the subject. 'Wish we weren't playing Harriet and Neil in the first round.'

'Do us good,' said Paddy. 'We know their weak points. We know we're better than they are. It'll give us confidence!' He gave me an encouraging smile as we went on. Harriet and Neil were already there.

'Just our luck having to play you two,' Harriet grumbled.

'Our sentiments precisely,' I said.

Actually, Paddy and I *are* good together – I'm reminded as soon as we start knocking up. He bounces around at the net but he always knows when to leave the shot for me. We always sense when one or other of us is tired or in need of a confidence boost. We get quite giggly sometimes. I can always make Paddy laugh. *Could* always – I haven't been so sure of him this week, as you know. Perhaps playing a match together will make everything all right again.

'Down the middle,' Paddy whispered, once we'd started. 'It works every time.' It was true. Neil and Harriet were fine at hitting the ball when it came into their court but very bad at knowing when to take or leave a shot. Harriet got riled if Neil poached and Neil got equally cross if he left it to Harriet and she didn't get to the ball. So playing down the middle shook up their personalities as well as their game. It wasn't long before they were barely speaking to each other and then only in monosyllables.

I enjoyed myself because it was a good hard-hitting game. I got a bit hot in the old tracksuit bottoms, but Paddy and I were beating them. Hardly anyone came to watch because they were all busy, though Phil and Kieron were spectators for five minutes or so. Kieron's presence didn't affect my game so long as I didn't think about the 'other stuff' (not even the word), and I was concentrating too hard on playing for that.

We won, of course. Paddy shook my hand and patted my back as you always do after a match. And then I couldn't help thinking about the 'other stuff'. I found myself looking at Neil in a different light when he did the same – after all, as I'd said to Lucy, everyone had to be fair game if the romance challenge was to come off. Neil's a mate, so I don't look at him critically usually – don't usually notice that he's got a terrible skin . . . Hey! This romance thing is not good! I don't want to notice bad things about my friends. Needless to say, I struck Neil off my list of potential romancers.

Back at the board, Paddy and I looked at how our Club had fared in the mixed. Lucy and Richard were through, though Rosie and Raj had been beaten by Claire and Robin. Lucy and Robin were busy congratulating one another at that very moment. Lucy came over and pulled me away from the crowd.

'I'm not going to give you a lift tonight!' she said.

'Why ever not?'

'Because you're going to go with your brother and *Kieron*. Remember?'

'Ssh! He'll hear.'

'He's not around – I checked.'

'Lucy – you won't tell anyone, will you?'

'Not even Robin.'

'Especially not Robin. And I don't want Paddy knowing either.'

'Ooh. Touchy. Don't worry, girlie, your secret's safe with me.'

'What secret?' asked Robin, coming to join us.

'Nothing you need worry your pretty little head about,' said Lucy, steering him away. 'Run along now Alex, and find your big brother.'

I stuck my tongue out at her. 'I'll get my coat,' I said, and went off to find Phil.

Phil and Kieron were playing a match. Mens' doubles. Great to watch. While I was waiting for them to finish, Megan came to join me with a guy I hadn't seen before: the famous Max. 'How did you get on?' I asked.

'We lost,' said Megan glumly, 'to Charlie and Louise Smart. They chewed us up and spat us out.'

'I'll tell you the good part, though,' said Max. 'We got a Smart invitation out of it. It was Charlie actually – when we were shaking hands he said to Louise that she ought to invite us to the barbecue tomorrow to kind of make up for totalling us. Nice guy, Charlie. Dead posh but doesn't act it. Anyway, Louise had to say yes. She must know everyone's heard it's a free-for-all.'

'Is it?' I said. 'I was always under the impression that the Smart set was rather exclusive.'

'Nah,' said Max. 'People like that love to feel they're at the centre of things. That's why they have parties. I'm going, for sure. And I'm making Megan come.'

'Well, I'll go if you go, Alex,' said Megan to me. 'Better still, you can give me a lift. Can I come round to yours first? I don't want to go home in between. I'd rather get Dad to take over for the whole evening.'

What could I say? 'OK,' I said weakly. People don't usually drop in to my house but I'm not used to being steamrollered like this.

'We're off now,' she said. 'In fact we're out of the tournament, but we're both coming to watch tomorrow. Nothing better to do. See you!'

So if it was to be Max, I'd see him again tomorrow and at the party. He might be just about possible if all my other attempts failed. What you'd call a fun guy. Hmm. But Phil and Kieron had just won. It was time to practise my charms on Kieron.

'Would you like to sit in the front, Alex?'

'Let Phil have a go. I don't mind going in the back with Kieron.'

Phil: 'Great, thanks. Don't mind if I do.'

Kieron: 'Are you sure, Alex? I'm a bit rank after that doubles match.'

Me: 'Well that makes two of us. My shirt's still superglued to my back.' *That's not very seductive.*

Then of course, Phil: 'Why didn't you take off your trousers if you were that hot?'

Me: silence. I'm desperate for something to say to

Kieron. Something with a hint of romance. Zoe, Lucy, where are you when I need you? I blink at him in a manner I imagine to be appealing.

'You OK, Alex? Something in your eye?'

'No. I'm fine. Ermm. Nice of you to ask.' I racked my brain for a compliment to pay him. 'I like your – your–' Everything he was wearing was quite unremarkable. But as he smiled I noticed that he had nice, even, white teeth. '–teeth.'

'Sorry, what was that?' Kieron asked. He laughed uproariously. 'It sounded as though you said "I like your teeth"!'

'No, silly!' I said. (Help, what could I substitute?) 'I said, "I like this seat!"'

'Good,' said Kieron. He gave me a funny sidelong look. 'But I'm afraid you're going to have to get out of it soon.'

'Why?' I asked, alarmed. Had I completely blown it? Was he ejecting me from his car?

'Because we're nearly home, klutz,' said Phil.

I'm not cut out for this, I'm really not. I rang Zoe to ask if I could back out of the deal, but she said absolutely no way. She was doing her best against the odds and I had to persevere too. She asked if I was all right and if I'd used up all the supplies yet. I said no, because I hadn't started, but I wished something would happen – I was getting terribly hot wearing trousers every day. That's what the emergency supplies are there for, birdbrain, she said. Use them just in case! It doesn't matter if you need them or not! Daft thing, keeping your long trousers on! See? This is the sort of stuff my Mum should have told me! Then I rang Lucy and told her how I had completely failed to entice Kieron. She said she'd meet me up at the Club tonight. Tomorrow we had an early start at the tournament because so many of the people still in – and that included both of us – had three matches to play.

'I can't do it, Lucy. I just don't know how to play this romance game. I did that fluttery eyelash thing that you do with Robin, and Kieron just asked if I had something in my eye. I mean, he was still nice to me, because he's a gent, basically, but he's starting to give me strange looks.'

We weren't even pretending to play tennis. Lucy'd had a more strenuous day than I had, but we were both saving ourselves for tomorrow.

'Let me think about it,' said Lucy. 'I'm sure we can come up with a plan. I'm trying to think what happened with Robin and me, but that was different because we simply fancied each other. We need a bit of a plan anyway, because tomorrow's long and complicated, isn't it? Three matches and a party.'

'Ten a.m. start. Do you realise I'm up against Louise Smartypants in every single semi-final?'

'At least we're *in* every single semi-final. Paddy too. The Club kicks ass again!' Lucy stood up and cheered. 'Actually, our lads don't have their semi-finals until Friday.'

'I've just remembered. Robin and Charlie can't play on Saturday, can they, because of the Prestige Gold Cup?'

'I know,' said Lucy. 'Robin feels terrible about it. He's really glad Paddy knocked him out now.'

'They're both still in the doubles and the mixed doubles. What'll they do? How are they going to get out of it?'

'Robin thinks the competition is better than them, but I'm not so sure. Nobody's better than Charlie in the under-16s. Their coach only sent them to get practice – he didn't think they'd get this far.'

It did seem unfair on our boys. And us, for that matter. 'The singles is the worst. Paddy has to beat Charlie to get into the final,' I said. 'And he's so desperate to win this year.'

'Maybe Charlie will lose on purpose.'

'That's almost as bad. Still, if he can't play on Saturday maybe he'll have to. Then it will be Paddy against Tom Smart for the final.'

'Ruddy Smarts. By the way, have you heard? Absolutely everybody's going to their barbecue tomorrow night. Sort of mass decision. People are just going to turn up.'

'I know. Even Megan and her friend Max. She wants to come back to my place first.'

'Lucky old her,' said Lucy. 'You don't usually let me in, however much I want to see the gorgeous Joel in his natural habitat.'

'Robin is a lot more gorgeous than Joel, believe me. And he doesn't put Domestos in his hair. I did try to put Megan off, but it didn't work. Means I'll have to introduce her to Mum and everything.'

'It's going to be so cool being at a party with Robin. Maybe you'll get somewhere with Kieron too. Nothing like a bit of fruit punch and a few burgers round the fire to get things moving.'

'Maybe.'

'Mum, would it be OK if I brought someone round tomorrow night between the tournament and going out to the Smarts' barbecue? Obviously you won't have to feed her.'

'Are you all going to this barbecue? Joel and Phil as well?'

'I expect so. I don't think there'll be a problem with lifts there and back.'

'Oh well. That's fewer people for supper then. Yes, dear. You know I like to meet your friends.'

Yes, but they're not that thrilled about meeting you. 'Thanks.'

A party and a romance. Who was it to be? Time was running out. Kieron was number one candidate. Who was number two? Max? Charlie? No. Not Charlie.

I had to make myself more attractive. To the old dressing-table on the landing. There are actually some odds and ends of make-up in there from the days when Mum wore it. Believe it or not, Joel and I used to play with it for dressing-up ten million years ago. I would enjoy reminding him of that one day. Yup – here it is. Little make-up bag with a Mary Quant daisy on it. Gosh, this takes me back. One lipstick. Mascara. Eyeshadow, green. Extremely small bottle of duty-free *Je Reviens* that must go back to the seventies at least. *Never mind*. I took the whole lot to my room and shut the door.

Now, my friends all wear make-up. Josie wears loads. Holly and Zoe probably do too, but they are more subtle. Lucy doesn't put it on most of the time, but she will if it's a party. Zoe's made me up once or twice for a laugh and it looked quite good.

I started with the lipstick. I didn't put much on, but I went over the edges so I still looked like a clown. Hey ho. Nothing ventured, nothing gained etc. He who dares . . . Then the eyeshadow. Green isn't really my colour. Doesn't go with sandy hair. Still. I just smoo-oothed a bit on. The light wasn't very good in my room. Never mind. This was just an experiment.

Then the mascara. It was ancient. I rattled the stick round the tube a few times. Right eye. Carefully does it. Fine. Left eye . . . Damn. I jabbed it in my eye by mistake. That made my eyes water and I blinked. A lot. Oh no. Now I had great black zigzags going down my face in rows. I looked like a whole troupe of clowns.

Knock knock.

'Don't come in! Who's that?'

'Kieron.'

Oh yeah? What sort of tricks was Joel playing on me? Maybe he'd like to be reminded right now of happier days playing with the make-up bag. Would he, huh. With a stream of expletives I hurled open the door.

'OK Joel, you *** scumbag! What is it this time, you *** toad?'

It *was* Kieron. I should have realised something was different. Joel wouldn't have waited for me to open the door.

Kieron did a sort of choke-hysteria giggle before returning to his gent-like ways and apologising – he thought he'd been directed to Phil's room. He was returning the sunglasses Phil had left in the car.

'No.' I acted all dignified and cool and stepped outside

my room. 'Phil's in here.' I knocked on Phil's door politely. Phil opened it, took one look at me and cracked up. Then he saw Kieron. 'What's going on?'

'These were in the car, mate,' said Kieron. 'One of the twins left off watching telly just long enough to open the door and tell me where I could find you.'

'More than one clown in this family, then,' said Phil, looking at me and doubling up again. 'Come in, big K. We don't often have visitors. Go and wash your face, Al. You look hideous.'

I kept thinking, *Kieron is here. Perhaps he really did come to see me. Perhaps Phil's sunglasses were just an excuse.*

'Let me come in too, Phil,' I asked. Perhaps someone as sophisticated as Kieron would be impressed by my enhanced beauty. I lowered the mascara-clogged eyelashes again.

Phil was not impressed. 'Only if you do something sensible with your face. I'm not having you embarrassing me in front of my friends.'

'Oh.' That said it, really. I didn't see Kieron objecting to Phil's high-handed behaviour on this occasion.

I slunk off to the bathroom, humiliated again. I locked the door, switched on the shaving light as well as the overhead one and inspected my face in the mirror. I did indeed look ridiculous. And Kieron had seen me looking like this. Sense of humour failure again. It's hard to make a joke about being seen looking completely batty by a guy you're trying to ensnare. *Give up Alex. Give up.*

Of course soap and water are barely adequate for removing large quantities of ancient mascara. Mysteriously there was some baby lotion in the bathroom cupboard, so that helped. Why can't my heap of a mum even do straightforward make-up things like other women? Has she no self-respect? Perhaps she doesn't like looking in the mirror. I'm beginning to know the feeling.

I slipped back into my room and pushed a pile of books up against the door. My gorilla grinned down at me. I ripped him off the wall. I moved my mirror into the light. I tied my hair back and clipped the straggly bits. Then I dipped my finger into the eyeshadow again and smeared just the tiniest bit on to my eyelids. I checked at every dab. A bit green (I could imagine Lucy saying that – It's OK Al, just a bit *green*). I applied the mascara again, ever so lightly – stroke – stroke – stroke – right eye. Stroke – stroke – stroke – left eye. I ignored the lipstick. I regarded myself in the mirror. *Not bad.* It wasn't bad. I'd try it. At the risk of further humiliation, I'd go downstairs like that.

I heard Kieron leave. He called out, 'Cheerio Alex!' as he went downstairs and I heard the twins letting him out. I went down. Everyone was milling around in the kitchen. The twins were hyped up from what they'd been watching on TV. Dad and Mum were involved in some gritted teeth wrangling, nothing unusual. Phil said, 'So what was all the face paint about?' but I said 'None of your business,' and turned to Joel instead. 'I suppose you've seen Tom Smart's hair?'

'Yeah, course,' said Joel. 'I helped him do it last night after *you* lot left me behind.'

And Mum said, 'Poor Joel, that really was too bad.'

Nobody mentioned my eyes.

*

Until later. My turn to help Mum tidy up the kitchen. What a surprise! 'I rather like your subtle eye make-up,' said Mum, noisily putting things away. 'I hardly noticed it at first, but that's the way it should be. My, my, how you're growing up all of a sudden.' She looked sad.

I was gobsmacked. 'Just experimenting,' I muttered.

'Oh, I recognise the make-up.'

'Sorry. I should have asked.'

'No, no! I kept it because you children used to love playing with it. Heavens, I've no time for make-up.'

'Why not, Mum?' I ventured.

She appeared not to hear me. But I'd just had a conversation with her! I went to bed feeling curiously elated. Despite everything.

WEDNESDAY

You and the opposition are two parts of a single whole.

EVENT/S	VENUE	WEATHER CONDITIONS	PHYSICAL HEALTH
U-16 singles	Mapledon	Grey, sunny later	Unpredictable
U-16 mixed			

Romance (have you ever heard of anything so daft?)

OPPONENT/VICTIM
Megan Birchill. Unusual unknown! I really liked her.
Neil and Harriet (I hate having to play other Club members).
Kieron (in the romance event).

TACTICS
None in the singles - should have had.
Mixed - played down the middle.
Romance - Blinked a lot. Paid compliments.

RESULT
Won
Won
Failed utterly.

EQUIPMENT

Dark tracksuit proved useful but hot. Know what to do now after talking to Zoe. Wish I'd realised before.

Ancient make-up (not so bad second time round).

COMMENTS

At least the mixed got sorted. Paddy almost back to his usual self once we were playing. That's what I've been missing! The old Paddy.

Megan is an amazing girl. She makes things happen.

Trying it on with Kieron was just so stupid. I'll have to think of someone else. Or give up.

TOMORROW'S MATCH

Singles, doubles and mixed doubles

Singles v Louise, worse luck.

Doubles v Louise and Claire, worse luck.

Mixed doubles v Alicia and bloke.

Lucy's got to play Alicia in the singles.

Paddy has a day off the singles before playing Charlie on Friday.

Smart barbecue and all that that entails.

Eight

I didn't feel too good on Thursday morning. My legs ached and my eyes felt gritty. I put it down to too much tennis and mucking about with mascara. Lucy picked me up at half past nine. On top of the early start, the prospect of *three* matches was almost more than I could bear. I'd taken Zoe's advice so at least I wouldn't be getting overheated.

'Well?' As soon as I got into the car Lucy twisted round to question me.

'Well what?' I replied blearily.

'Kieron!' she hissed. 'What are you going to do today?'

'Nothing at all,' I said. 'He came round last night.'

'Wow! I didn't think you had visitors.'

'We don't. He was dropping something off for Phil.'

'Bet that was just an excuse.'

'Unlikely, but even if it was, the sight of me with weird make-up all over my face didn't exactly bowl him over.'

'How did that happen?'

'He knocked on my bedroom door thinking it was Phil's, and I let him in, thinking it was one of the boys winding me up. Trouble was, I'd just been experimenting with Mum's old make-up and blinked mascara all over my face – as well as bright red lipstick.'

'Mmm. Attractive.'

'Exactly. I'm giving up on Kieron. I might want to keep him up my sleeve for a few years' time.'

'So who are you going to have your romance with?'

'I don't feel like having a romance with anyone. I feel lousy today for some reason. Three matches will keep me busy. Maybe I'll have thought of another victim by tonight.'

'I'm looking forward to tonight.'

'I'm not. I'm only going because Megan has bulldozed me into it.'

Lucy and I were soon started on our singles semi-finals. Although it was an early start for the under-16s and there weren't many spectators, we had proper umpires and there were some local reporters and photographers around. Dad makes it to the Friday afternoon semi-finals – under-18s and boys (unfair), and of course he makes it to Finals Day whether we're in it or not, but he couldn't come today. Joel threatened to make an appearance in the afternoon, but I can't say I was particularly thrilled about that.

Lucy looked tiny as she followed Alicia to their court. Both Alicia and her cousin Connie are close to six foot. And professional-looking. I didn't envy Lucy.

I didn't envy myself much, either. Two matches against Louise Smart in a day, and a third in the offing. I'd be gutted if she won all of them, though it wouldn't surprise me. Whatever you think of the Smarts, they are ace tennis players. I expect even Scarlett totes a little tennis racquet about – and beats the other three-year-olds into the ground.

Louise looked the business this morning. Her gear was brand new and she wore her hair tightly pulled back. Her bottom waggled even more bossily than usual. I noticed that she wore eyeliner and lipstick. 'Are you ready, Alexandra?' she asked, condescendingly I thought. But I wasn't going to let her win before we'd begun.

'Oh, more than!' I replied more enthusiastically than I felt. 'I've been looking forward to this match.' (Dad's training – *never act defeated. Even when you're one set and 4–5 down, there's still a possibility of winning* – it was also today's handy hint in the tennis diary.)

Actually, at one set and 4–5 down, there didn't seem much chance of me still beating Louise Smart. I'd given her a good run for her money, but I wasn't on top form today. She won 7–5 6–4. A respectable score, but annoying all the same. She isn't necessarily better than me.

Lucy appeared, looking distinctly hacked off. Her

thumbs down gesture confirmed that she'd lost, too. To make matters worse, the organisers wanted to start the girls' doubles semi-finals as soon as possible – the boys were already playing their third round, and that way we'd all be free for the mixed in the afternoon.

We made our way to the clubhouse. I wasn't going to miss out on my loser's drink. I needed it. Lucy sat with us without saying anything, her mood made even blacker when Claire turned up all fresh and keen. She couldn't really forgive Claire for being Robin's partner. Claire's OK actually. 'Hi guys!' she said. 'Are we all ready to play? They want us to start as soon as possible.'

'Don't you think we ought to pace ourselves?' I asked. 'We've all got mixed doubles matches after this.'

Claire was ready to agree, but Louise had other ideas. 'The mixed isn't really important, is it?' she said.

'Thanks a bunch,' retorted Claire. 'You're only playing me and Robin.'

'Just a bit of fun,' said Louise briskly. 'I want to finish everything and get home as soon as possible. We've got this barbecue tonight.'

'I know. Thank you for inviting us,' I said wickedly.

'Really looking forward to it,' Lucy added, perfectly aware that Louise could hardly say she didn't want us to come.

'So we'll go and check in, shall we?' said Louise.

'I suppose so. You do it. We'll see you in ten minutes, OK?' I wanted to talk tactics with Lucy.

'I haven't even had a chance to find Robin this morning,' Lucy wailed. 'My match with Alicia was awful. I never even got going.'

'Mine wasn't much fun either.'

'You looked as if you were winning yours. I didn't realise Louise had beaten you at first.'

'Well, she did. And I don't want her winning again. So we've got to play on Claire. She's surprisingly steady, but nowhere as good as Louise.'

'I expect they'll be playing on me.'

'We won't give them a chance. Come on, Luce. It's a challenge. You know me and challenges.'

'Don't I just. Except that you've given up on Kieron.'

'Not for ever! Just for now. And I have others lined up.'

'OK. Club members rise to the challenge! I won't let you down if you don't let me down.'

We lost to Claire and Louise too. 6–3 6–3. It was all over in under an hour.

In disgust, Lucy and I went to the farthest possible court to rake over our woes. 'Oh well,' she said. 'Sorry partner, and all that. You deserved better.'

'They were going to win, whatever. Think of it as conserving energy. At least no one saw us.'

'I console myself with the thought that the fewer matches I'm in, the more time I have with Robin.'

'So what *are* Robin and Charlie going to do after Friday? D'you think they will lose on purpose? Paddy would be so gutted if he only won because his opponent let him.'

'Well, only one couple can go through in the mixed. Where are they in the doubles?'

'I know they're not in the same half of the draw as Paddy and Richard.'

'So it's quite possible that Charlie might be in all three semi-finals.'

'Or Robin in two and Charlie in two,' I said. 'I'm sure the organisers wouldn't be very happy about this if they knew.'

'Well we're not the ones to tell them.'

There was nothing anyone could do about it now. In the distance two people were walking towards us, Megan striding and Max bounding along beside her. They threw themselves down on the grass next to us.

'So you're the famous Max are you?' said Lucy with a wry look at me.

'How's it going then?' said Megan, not giving Max a chance to reply. 'Got my party gear in my bag.' She patted it. 'I know I could have worn what I'm wearing now, but I like tarting myself up and Dad's given me the evening off. Still OK if I come to yours, Alex?'

'Yes, fine,' I said weakly. 'Actually, the day has been poor, so far, hasn't it Lucy? We've both lost two matches.'

'I don't hold out much hope for this afternoon either,' said Lucy. 'Robin and I are against Connie and partner and Al and Paddy are against Alicia and hers.'

'Who are Connie and Alicia?' asked Max.

'The Venus and Serena Williams of Mapledon,' said Lucy despondently.

'Oh yes, I've seen them,' said Max. 'Why are you both so gloomy?'

'I don't know,' I said. 'Losing might have something to do with it.'

'Hormones, probably,' said Max sagely.

'And what would you know about hormones?' Megan asked him.

'I might be male, but I too have hormones,' said Max. 'Anyway, I spent ten days cooped up with a whole load of girls recently. I understand these things.'

I kept quiet. What if he was right?

'Can we move on to more cheerful matters please,' said Megan, 'such as which matches to watch this afternoon?'

'Well, all the under-18s are pretty good at this stage. Or under-16 boys' doubles – you could watch any of the boys from the Club, they're all likely to win today's matches and go on to the semi-final tomorrow.'

'Why aren't you watching them?' asked Max. He had a bright, intent look which I actually found quite appealing (but, oh dear, not romantic. Try, Alex. *Try*.).

'We're sick of tennis!' I said. 'When you've lost two matches and you're contemplating losing a third you go off it a bit.'

Max stood up. 'I'm going to have a wander round. Does anyone want to come with me?'

Lucy raised her eyebrows at me. She tilted her head in Max's direction. It was the most animated I'd seen her all day. I really didn't feel like moving, but the word 'challenge' kept haunting me, and Lucy wasn't going to let me off the hook. 'I'll come with you, Max,' I said. 'I've played in the Mapledon tournament practically all my life so I ought to know my way around.'

The first match we sat in on was Phil and Kieron. 'That's my brother playing there – one of them. His partner's called Kieron. Kieron's nice, but I don't really want to see him right now.'

We moved on. *Great.* There was Joel watching us with a sneaky grin on his face. I'd forgotten he was coming. 'Aren't you going to introduce me to your friend, little sis? Is this who the OTT make-up was for? Phil and Kieron were telling me about it on the way here.'

I blushed. Horrible brothers. 'Max this is Joel. Joel this is Max.' I hastily led Max on.

'What was all that about? Could this have something to do with why you don't want to see Kieron?'

'Oh, just my nasty brother trying to embarrass me.'

'Looks as though he succeeded.'

'He always does.'

All four matches for the under-16 boys' doubles were being played on adjacent courts. There was a lot of interest. Paddy and Richard were winning. 'Who's the guy at the net this end?' asked Max. 'He's so speedy.'

'That's my partner, Paddy Gardner,' I said. I felt quite proud. 'And Richard, Lucy's partner.'

Max watched a bit more. 'Is Paddy tipped to win the under-16s?'

'He'd love to,' I said, 'but see what you think of the competition. It's good to hear what an outsider thinks. Paddy's got to play Charlie in the semis and if he gets through that he'll either have to play Leon – that guy serving over there (brother of the famous Connie), or Tom Smart (whose barbecue you're going to tonight).'

Max watched all the contenders carefully. 'I would have thought Charlie was the only one who'd give him any grief. Is he really under sixteen?'

'Yup. Not fair is it?'

Max watched some more. 'Though I would say, his

left knee is giving him just a tiny bit of trouble. Watch him run. There! See what I mean?'

He was right. The slightest of movements to save that knee. Charlie was a joy to watch anyway – he had a distinctive way of spreading the fingers of his left hand as he hit the ball. It was almost like watching a dancer. Hang on, I hate Charlie. Charlie jeered at me with Joel.

Charlie spotted me. He waved as if nothing was wrong between us, as if I hadn't been avoiding him or blanking him for a day and a half. He even mouthed something at me, but it was unintelligible over that distance, and I wasn't going any closer. If it was that important, he knew he could get a message to me via Robin and Lucy.

'So Phil and Joel are your brothers. Paddy and Richard are yours and Lucy's partners. Kieron is someone you don't want to see. Charlie is someone you obviously don't want to talk to, even though *his* partner has something going with *your* partner . . . There's more than meets the eye at this tennis tournament – real "mixed doubles". You must fill me in some time!'

We sat down where we could watch the four matches that were all in their finishing stages. 'So what about you and Megan? I only met her yesterday, but I like her.'

'Well, first of all, there is nothing whatsoever between us. I'm not in her league.'

'What do you mean?'

'Megan, as you've probably noticed, is kind of larger than life. Her Mum died when she was about ten, and she more or less brings up the two younger ones. They're off on playschemes this week – that's why she's high as a kite to be out of the house. School holidays are a complete pain for her.'

'I didn't know.'

'Why should you?'

'It's just that I hear something like that and it makes my problems pale into insignificance. I can't imagine actually having to *look after* my brothers.' I glanced at my watch. 'Max, I'm going to get called quite soon. But before we go – you are going to be at the barbecue tonight, aren't you?'

'Sure thing.'

'I'll tell you more about the complications then. And Max?'

'Uh-huh?'

'Since you're such a great guy I might just have to ask you to do me a *massive* favour. I won't tell you what it is now, because it might not happen. But be prepared. OK?'

Lucy and Megan were approaching. I slipped away. I felt rather sick – I thought a solitary muffin and a cup of tea might help.

I sat myself in a corner of the clubhouse and prayed that no one, e.g. Ethlie, would come and bother me. I didn't want to lose a third match or let Paddy down but I had a really unpleasant pain in the pit of my stomach. Nerves probably. I made myself invisible and watched the world go by. There was a lot of activity round the board as the semi-finals took shape. Joel came and studied it for a while but he didn't notice me. The first mixed doubles matches were called as the other doubles players came off. I was lucky to have as much time as I did between matches. Mrs Smart appeared, looking queenly, and there was a sort of buzz round her for a while in anticipation of the barbecue. Scarlett was with her. She spotted me and ran over. 'Are you going to come to my party tonight?' she asked me and I just had time to tell her I was before her mother hauled her off again.

'P. Gardner and Miss A. Dunbar; L. Johnson and Miss A. Smith. To the desk please.' That was us.

'Hi there,' said Paddy. 'I wondered where you'd got to.'

Dad: Never let your partner think you're below par. 'I was preparing myself for the big match. You know, carbohydrates, feet up, positive thinking.'

'Great. Because we're going to win this one aren't we?' Paddy's learnt the same rules as I have, but I actually detected a look of concern in his eyes. Alicia and partner arrived. They both wore baseball caps and carried cyclists' bottles of water – very professional. We went over to warm up – not that Paddy needed to. As on other days the sun had broken through the clouds during the afternoon and it was quite hot. I took off my tracksuit before we started. (Thank you Zoe.) Paddy was on a roll. I felt reassured but also determined to keep him on this winning streak.

It was a tough game. Like Max, Alicia's partner had only been brought in for the mixed doubles. He was a flashy player – daunting at first, but comparatively easy to beat because he so often fluffed his shots and then ran through the gamut of self-hate moves. He threw his racquet to the ground several times, hit the ball hard against the wire mesh, cursed himself – all of which made the two of us feel more in control. I was aware of Paddy covering me, though. He didn't leave as many shots for me as he might have done, spared me from running across the court behind him. He's psychic, that guy! And never, ever a cross word. Only encouragement and praise. I mean, I do the same for him, but during that match I really appreciated it.

Towards the end my friends came to watch. Lucy's mum was there, so I knew our lift was in place as soon as we finished. I was less pleased to see Joel and Phil and Kieron amongst the spectators, but luckily by that time we were 4–2 up in the second set, with the first set in the bag. I couldn't have borne to go on to three sets.

'Vultures are gathering,' said Paddy as he came back to receive.

'It's the barbecue they're gathering for,' I said.

Alicia served a double fault. 'You are coming, aren't you?' I asked Paddy as we moved again. It would be a shame if he wasn't there.

'Not sure,' said Paddy from the net. We played a long point which Paddy won with a terrific cross-court volley. He walked back. 'I don't know all those people.'

'Rubbish! You know them as well as I do. You *know me*!' The game got tricky at that moment. If we got to deuce and they won it, we'd only be 4–3 up – a dangerous score. 'I'll shut up,' I said, remembering uncomfortably Max and the massive favour. Maybe I wouldn't want Paddy as an audience.

'Yeah, let's WIN,' said Paddy.

Six points later we had. But as we were shaking hands I suddenly knew I had to rush to the loo. I couldn't hang around to see whether or not Paddy was coming to the barbecue, I just had to get to the clubhouse. Megan, anxious about her lift, followed me.

'You OK?' she asked from the next cubicle.

'No,' I said. And then, 'Well, I'm fine really. I've just started my period. Good job I came prepared.'

Nine

I wasn't sure how Megan would react to my bizarre household. Seriously, I always visit my friends – I never bring them home. Maybe it's something to do with having an enormously fat mother. So I couldn't have been more surprised when Megan announced in her Janet Street-Porter voice as soon as we got in the door – 'What an amazing house! Doesn't it smell nice? – all lemony and clean! Ours always stinks of frying and cat food.'

Mum hove into view. 'This is Megan, Mum.' I wanted to fill Mum in on the facts I'd learned about Megan, but it didn't seem appropriate.

'Great house, Mrs Dunbar,' said Megan enthusiastically. 'Really *homely*.'

'I'll take Megan up to my room,' I said, not wanting to expose her to the twins or Joel.

Too late, because Jack came down the stairs, deep in a Nintendo game. 'What's for supper, Mum?' he said, not lifting his eyes.

'Chilli con carne,' she replied.

'Aw,' said Jack. 'That means it'll be spicy doesn't it?'

'It'll be chilli con carne, yes,' said Mum.

'Can I have a sandwich?' he whined.

'Ooh!' Megan couldn't keep quiet. 'Hope you're not going to let him get away with *that*, Mrs Dunbar!'

Jack was silenced. Mum, already on her way to make him a sandwich, looked back, surprised.

'Sorry,' said Megan. 'None of my business, but I bawl mine out if they moan about the food.'

'Oh,' said Mum, flummoxed. 'It's just that Jack makes such a mess when he does his own sandwiches–'

'Come on, Megan,' I said. 'We don't have a lot of time.' She followed me up the stairs past Jack, who flattened himself against the wall with a look of something like respect on his face.

'Sorry,' she said, once we were in my room. 'Forgot you probably want to get to the bathroom. I get hideous periods. Do you?'

'Um. I don't know. This is my first one.'

'What? Oh, wow! Congratulations! Welcome to the world of womanhood!'

'That's how my friend Zoe put it,' I said, and suddenly burst into tears.

Megan sat on the bed beside me. 'Oh bad luck. It's not very good timing is it? Still, that's typical. Have to get used to it.'

I couldn't stop crying.

'Hey! There, there.'

I carried on snivelling. Poor Megan didn't know quite what to do. 'Won't be a minute,' she said, and then, to my horror I heard her running down the stairs, calling, 'Mrs Dunbar? Mrs Dunbar? I think your daughter needs you!'

Joel: 'So what's up with poor little Ally Wallie?'

Megan: 'Girl stuff. Where's your mum?'

Joel: 'Arranging the cushions at right-angles probably. What sort of girl stuff?'

Megan: 'None of your business.'

Joel (retaliating sarcastically): 'Sorry I asked.'

And then there were muffled females voices followed by Megan taking the stairs three at a time and Mum huffing and puffing behind her. And then they were both in my room.

Mum came and sat on my bed too. (She's so heavy I boinged up in the air a couple of inches.) 'Darling,' she said. 'Why didn't you say?'

'It only just happened, didn't it?' Megan said, genuinely excited on my behalf.

'I've had some supplies ready for you for a while,' said Mum. 'I'll go and fetch them. I've got some of those little disposal bags that you can buy these days, too. You'll want to be a bit discreet in this house full of boys.' And she shuffled out.

Far from easing up, I was now crying buckets.

'Are you in pain?' asked Megan.

'No!' I sobbed. 'It's complicated. I don't usually get on with my mum.'

'Well start getting on with her. At least you've got one.'

'I know,' I hiccupped.

Joel knocked on the door and put his head round immediately.

'What's going on?' he asked. Joel doesn't like not knowing what's going on.

'I told you before!' said Megan. 'It's none of your business. Go away!' I sobbed afresh. 'How did he earn his cool reputation, your brother? He's about as sensitive as a rhinoceros.'

'And that's unfair on rhinoceroses,' I managed a laugh.

'Hey, that's better!' said Megan.

Mum rustled in with a large Boots plastic carrier containing a brand-new sponge bag and much the same variety of things as Zoe had given me, as well as a little swing-top bin and a pack of scented purple plastic bags.

'Mum – why didn't you tell me you'd got all this stuff?'

She sighed. 'I didn't want to presume – or pry,' she said defensively. 'Anyway, here you are. Your friend Megan is probably more use to you now than I am. I must go and get on with that chilli.'

'That the boys don't want,' I said under my breath as she left.

'Why is she so fat?' asked Megan in her upfront way.

'Dunno,' I said. 'She wasn't always like that. Not in the photos.'

'Right, let's get ready,' said Megan. 'What are you wearing? My tennis gear's rubbish but I've got good party clothes. I've brought loads, so you can borrow something if you want.'

'Nothing pale,' I said.

'Oh, don't be ridiculous! Nothing much will happen if this is your first time. Anyway, that's what all this stuff your mum gave you is for. Remember that a quarter of the girls at the barbecue, not to mention the tennis tournament, will be in the same boat.'

'Yuk!'

'True. Though it might be an idea not to swim.'

'So how do you explain to people that you're not going in the pool?'

'*If* they're rude enough to ask, you simply give them a withering look and say, "Why do you think?", and if they still insist on not understanding, tell them, in gory detail. OK. Now, you'd look good in this little number.'

Half an hour later we sashayed downstairs. I was wearing a red-and-gold shot top of Megan's with a pair of her baggy trousers. She'd pinned my hair up and made up my face a little. I felt pretty cool. She looked much the same in a black-and-silver top.

'I've got some money for burgers,' said Megan. 'Have you got a corner shop?'

I hadn't thought of that – I wondered if the boys had. We went into the kitchen where Mum was ironing Joel's T-shirt while Joel looked on.

'Mum – we all ought to take something for the barbecue. If you give me some money I'll buy something for Phil and Joel as well.'

'Spare ribs for me,' said Joel.

'You'll have what I choose,' I retorted, 'unless you want to buy it yourself.'

Mum fetched her purse and gave me a tenner. 'I'll want change,' she said.

'Don't worry Mrs Dunbar,' said Megan. 'I'm the burger expert. It's what my lot get most days.'

'Doesn't your mother–' *Oh Mum, please stop right there!*

'She died,' said Megan, matter-of-factly. 'But Dad's feeding them tonight. I've got the night off! Ta-ra!'

My dad was just letting himself in when we got back. Joel looked at his watch. 'We ought to be off, Dad.'

'Give me a chance to turn round,' said Dad. Then he saw us. 'Hey, you two girls look nice. Anyone seen Alex anywhere?'

'Not funny, Dad. This is my friend Megan.'

'Hi,' said Megan.

Mum appeared with a coolbag to put all our burgers in. Dad gave her a kiss. 'Sometimes I wish you could drive, dear,' he said. 'I'm almost too tired to be a taxi-driver tonight.'

'Doesn't Philip drive yet?' asked Megan. 'I can't wait – only eighteen months to go! You ought to learn, Mrs D. I know the *best* driving instructor. Are we off then? Bye! Thanks for having me!'

Everyone was at the Smarts'. Tuesday night's swim seemed a long time ago, and I felt kind of safe with Megan. She gave me courage. It was even quite nice to arrive with Phil and Joel – people are pleased to see them.

Louise and Claire both leapt on Joel. 'Hey this is some party,' he said, making them titter (why?) and they marched him off for a swim.

'Airheads,' muttered Megan.

'You're not very impressed by my brother, are you?' I asked her.

'Not by that one,' she said, 'but I quite like this one!' She beamed at Phil, making him blush. 'Though I happen to know that a certain young lady named Lana is expected tonight . . . which means I won't get a look-in.' Phil blushed some more.

'How on earth did you know that?'

'Oh, I keep my ear to the ground,' Megan said. 'I'd better go and find Max. Hi, Kieron. You're looking very fine tonight!' And she was off into the throng.

Phil's eyes were darting around nervously. 'Lana's here, mate – allegedly,' he said by way of apology to Kieron.

'Go seek out the lovely Lana!' said Kieron. 'I'll content myself with the lovely Alexandra. How you doin' Al?'

'Fine,' I said.

'You look every inch a babe tonight.'

'You flatter me.'

'So the other night was just a rehearsal, was it?'

'In a manner of speaking.'

I was still hanging on to our coolbag with the burgers in, and Kieron was also clutching a carrier bag. 'Shall we go and dump these somewhere?' he suggested, and I followed him to the major (Scout camp size) barbecue that had been set up on the patio. We each grabbed a can of Coke while we were at it. We sat down together on a garden bench. 'So who's the lucky guy?' he asked. 'The one the rehearsal was for? You certainly got it right this evening – the hair, everything!'

'Kieron, you're so nice to me. Why?'

'Why not, kiddo? Two years' time. It's a date, OK? Even if I have to fight off the competition.'

'OK, if you say so.'

Kieron leant over and kissed me on the cheek just as a stunning redhaired girl came over to us. He stood up to greet her. 'Ingrid, hi!' And they went off arm in arm, leaving me to put my hand up to my cheek. So that was Kieron well and truly off the list.

Where were Lucy, Max, Robin, Charlie even? Where

was Paddy? It was time to investigate. I wandered towards the swimming pool, trying to put the other night to the back of my mind. I wasn't going to be beaten by Joel. At the gate Scarlett and her little friend spotted me. 'There she is! Will you come and play that game with us again? Please? Please?'

'Sorry guys. I've come to party tonight, not swim.'

'Aw.'

Joel appeared, dripping. 'Not coming in this time then Alex? Scarlett wants you to.'

'No,' I said. 'I told them I'm here to party tonight. Don't feel like getting wet.'

Claire and Louise appeared behind him. 'Why don't you want to swim, Alex?' he persisted now he had an audience.

'Why do you think?' I retorted on cue.

'Honestly, Joel,' said Louise. 'You're hopeless.' They were tittering again, but I had won. I held my ground and watched the swim for a while. Scarlett and friend had found another victim – though they weren't having nearly as much fun as they did with me. I felt quite calm for the first time in ages. Max would probably say it was hormones.

Calm, but hungry. Smells from the barbecue were wafting over – if my friends had any sense they were loading their plates with food. I was right. Lucy saw me and called me over to join her in the queue. Her, Robin – and Charlie. I didn't know what to say to Charlie. Lucy and Robin were chattering so much it didn't show at first – I talked to Lucy, and Charlie talked to Robin. We got through platefuls of food that way. I was even enjoying myself – just so long as Lucy and Robin stayed.

But they didn't stay. One of those irresistible dance songs floated over to us and Lucy hauled Robin to his feet and whisked him away. I was left with Charlie.

Charlie: 'It's taken me until now to realise why you weren't talking to me.'

Me: 'Well.'

Charlie: 'I wasn't laughing at you the other night.'

Me: 'What were you laughing at then?'

Charlie sensed that I was lightening up. I was. 'Oh I don't know. Joel's like you – he's funny, but that was uncalled for. I think I was laughing because someone had farted or something. Nothing to do with Joel. You know I tried to ring you later on, don't you?'

'Lucy told me, yes.'

'Robin and I had decided to ask you two to be our partners in the mixed doubles. You and Paddy hadn't signed up at the time, if you remember,' he added carefully, 'so it seemed like a good idea.'

'OK, OK.'

'So you're not cross any more?'

'No.'

'Phew. Shall we go in there and leap about with the others?'

'OK. Charlie? There's something I want to ask you before we go in where it's noisy.'

'Fire away.'

'Does everyone know that you won't be playing on Saturday?'

'We're not exactly shouting it from the rooftops.'

'So what's going to happen in your semi-finals? Are you going to lose them on purpose?'

'I'm assuming that the eventual finalists will be better than me.'

'But they're not, are they? Paddy, for one, would hate it if he felt you'd *let* him win.' Just the thought of Paddy's hurt pride really upset me.

'I suppose I hadn't thought of it in terms of individuals. Jeez – Louise and I are playing you and Paddy together aren't we?'

'Yup.'

'Actually that's not a problem. You'll win that.'

'What do you mean? Louise beat me today.'

'Maybe, but she's no better than you–' I started to protest. '–No she isn't, you know. I've watched you both, and I know these things. And–' he carried on as I started to protest again, 'you and Paddy are a fantastic partnership. You work really well together. Louise and I don't know each other at all. And though I'm good at the net,' he bragged, 'Louise isn't.'

'So you think we can beat you on merit?'

'I do.'

'Good. You'd better watch out then. What about the boys' doubles?'

'Robin's not as good as I am. Neil and Raj can win if they play on him ruthlessly.'

'Poor Robin!'

'Who do you want to win this match?'

'OK. But the one I'm really worried about is Paddy.' *Where was he?*

'I'm really worried about him too. I think he's going to beat me.'

'What's the order of play?'

'I think they'll let us do the singles while we're fresh.

Probably mixed doubles last.' He stood up. 'Come on. You haven't made me laugh once this evening. Let's have a dance. Then I can make you laugh.'

It was dark and heaving in the room with the music: a converted garage – usually a games room with a table tennis table, Charlie told me. Phil and Kieron were in there with Lana and Ingrid. Joel had gone for Claire – which showed good taste on his part but not on hers. Even Ethlie was jigging away on her own. I like dancing, so long as it doesn't get smoochy. Eek. No. I couldn't do the romance thing with Charlie. Almost, But not. Almost – but how could I kiss someone if I didn't want to? It all seemed so alien. And where was Paddy?

I was saved from a slow number by the arrival of Max. Excitable Max with *bleached* hair! 'Your turn Charlie!' he said. 'What do you think of mine, eh?'

'What's going on?' I asked.

'Tom's got a production line going,' said Max. He did a twirl. 'Cool, or what?'

'Can't wait,' said Charlie and set off up the stairs.

'Scalp feels a bit tender,' said Max. 'Can we go outside in the fresh air? I think the fumes are making my eyes water.'

'Is Megan having hers done too?'

'No, she's just an onlooker. She said to tell you that's where she was.'

'It's quite cold out here, Max. Hang on while I get my jacket will you. I won't be a sec.'

'I'll be here, don't you worry,' said Max, seating himself on a fancy 'love seat' the Smarts had placed in a herb garden beyond the pool.

My bag was upstairs so I visited the bathroom where

the hair colouring was taking place. Much hilarity as Charlie stripped his top off ready to be the next sacrificial victim and presented his glossy brown locks for bleaching. Megan waved from the thick of it.

Max was waiting for me. You can guess what favour I wanted to ask him. My romance pledge was unfulfilled and I had this feeling Max and I could concoct something together that I could use to convince the others. 'OK sweetie, what is it?' said Max, running his hand through his hair in a camp way as I sat round from him in the love seat. In fact it was a sort of double love seat, made in the shape of a curved '3' rather than an 'S'. I was in the middle.

'Just listen then.'

'I'm all yours.'

'I made a sort of pact with three friends that each of us would have a holiday romance and report back on it. Only – I haven't had one. I'm useless at that sort of thing.'

At that moment Deathly Ethlie burst on the scene. 'Oh there you are, Alex!' she said, gripping my arm. 'I haven't seen you for ages!'

'I'm kind of in the middle of something at the moment, Ethlie. Can I catch up with you later?'

'Oh no! Really?' she said, predictably. 'All right then,' and wandered off, laughing.

'Did you say something funny just then?' said Max.

'No, she always says that.'

'So how can I help you with your romance?' Max leered at me. 'Do you want us to be caught snogging or something? I'm game.'

'No!'

'Well what, then? Just a quick kiss? Naked? In the parents' bedroom?'

'Max!' I thumped him.

'You've never kissed anyone have you?'

'I—'

'Go on, I can tell.'

'All right. No. I haven't. There seems to be too much spit involved.'

'Tell you what. I'll teach you an actor's trick a friend showed me. It looks as though you're kissing but actually you put your hand in the way.'

'Show me.'

He grabbed the back of my head with one hand, put the other one over my mouth and pretended to kiss me passionately. It felt strange, especially as I was nearly overwhelmed by the smell of bleach. 'Excellent. Do you want to go and try it out on the dance floor?'

'Not yet.'

'You mean there's more? What else do you want me to do? No one's ever asked me to pretend to have a romance before. I could hold your hand?' He picked up my hand and stroked it. It tickled. 'Rip my clothes off?' He pulled his bleach-spattered T-shirt over his head. 'You could lie with your head in my lap – actually, no, that's not such a good idea.'

'I don't know. You see, that's the problem, I don't know what I have to do.'

'Hey!' Max was momentarily distracted. 'Here comes Charlie boy – a very fetching blond!'

Charlie strode out to the love seat. 'What do you think?'

'Cool,' we both said as he sat on my other side.

'What are you two up to?'

'I'm teaching her to kiss,' said Max.

'You *what*?' Charlie sounded quite shocked.

'Let's show him,' said Max. And so we went through the whole drama for him.

'That was useless!' said Charlie. 'I could see your hand! This is how you should do it!' And, from the other side of the love seat he put one hand behind my head – and the other in my hair – and kissed me for real!

'Mmmmmuh – mmmmmuh!' I said struggling. 'You weren't supposed to do it *really*.'

'Oh well, if he's allowed to do it unprotected, then so am I,' said Max, and grabbed my head again.

'Oy!' yelled Charlie, 'I was enjoying that!' and tried to pull me back again.

At which point Megan arrived. 'Hey guys!' she said. 'Look who I've just found wandering around like a lost sheep.'

It was Paddy. But all we saw was his retreating back, and all we heard was his diminishing voice saying, 'I knew I shouldn't have come.'

Ten

I tried ringing Paddy as soon as Dad had driven us home (he didn't want Phil and me having a late night before semi-finals day, though I could have slept in until lunch time if I'd wanted). I wasn't sure what I was going to say to Paddy, but his mum answered and said that he'd gone to bed early on account of having three big matches the next day. She sounded proud.

THURSDAY

Never act defeated. Even when you're one set and 4–5 down, there's still a possibility of winning.

EVENT/S	VENUE	WEATHER CONDITIONS	PHYSICAL HEALTH
U-16 singles			
U-16 doubles	Mapledon	Warm	Curse, lousy
U-16 mixed			
Smart barbecue	Smart Towers		

OPPONENT/VICTIM
Louise Smart
Ditto and Claire.
Alicia and Luke
Kieron, Max, Charlie, Paddy - you name them.

TACTICS
None really.
None really.
None really.
Romance - Tried to get Max to pretend to have a romance with me.

RESULT
Lost
Lost
Won
Confusion

EQUIPMENT
Emergency supplies came in handy.
Megan's make-up and clothes.

COMMENTS
Too much to fit in here. Extraordinary day all round. Mum actually nice to me.

TOMORROW'S MATCH
Mixed doubles v Louise Smart and Charlie.
Paddy's big match against Charlie.

I lay awake for ages thinking about the weird day I'd had. First period. First kiss. Practically the first time I'd had a sympathetic conversation with Mum.

Kissing Charlie – which was *very* different from pretending to kiss Max – was all mixed up in my mind with Paddy turning up. In fact, as I drifted into a sleep that bristled with vivid dreams, Paddy was the one I was kissing. And then I'd jerk awake and sit up, trembling, every second and every centimetre of Charlie's soft lips on mine replaying itself. His face tilted and his eyelids closed in slow motion. The slight bristle of his chin grazed for an eternity. The awkwardness of our teeth briefly clashing lasted for excruciating aeons. (Not to mention the strong smell of bleach – it'll probably be linked with kissing for the rest of my life.) Then me, struggling to get away. Pathetic, naive girl. What must they think of me? It was only a bit of fun.

What had Paddy seen? Why did he act so – *hurt*? The others wondered what had happened to Paddy's sense of humour, but I know Paddy's got a great sense of humour.

'I think he's jea-lous,' Megan had said to me in a sing-song voice.

'What of?' I'd said.

'You tell me-he,' she'd said, in the same tone as before.

And then, before anything at all was resolved, there was Dad, car keys at the ready, prising Phil away from Lana, Joel away from Claire and me away from my group of friends.

'See you tomorrow,' said Charlie, cheerful and completely unfazed. Kissing was clearly just another game to him.

'We'll try and come on Saturday, won't we Max?' said Megan. 'Though I might have to bring one of the kids.' She gave me a hug. 'Good luck with – everything! Be nice to Paddy. I sense that something's going on behind those gorgeous deep blue eyes of his.'

All their words were going round and round in my head. I had to get to sleep – tomorrow's match was important. I really couldn't let Paddy down now. It all meant too much to him. And I had to be there for his match against Charlie. Ah. I didn't want to think about that. What if Charlie played badly on purpose and Paddy thought I'd put him up to it?

In the small hours I got up quietly to fetch some water and go to the loo. Mum appeared from nowhere. Scary because she's so huge. 'Everything all right, love?'

'Yeah, fine thanks, Mum,' and then she slip-slopped off back to bed. It was as if she had been acting on instinct.

I went to sleep after that.

'Nice girl, Megan,' Mum said, as she handed me my sandwiches in the morning. 'Fancy having to look after her family like that – she's only a kid herself.'

'Doesn't seem to get her down,' I said. Kieron was at the door to pick us up.

'Seems there were two lucky guys last night, then,' Kieron said to me.

'Oh shut up, Kieron, we were only mucking about.'

'Didn't ruin your make-up then?'

'What's all this?' said Phil, climbing into the car after me.

'Idle gossip,' I said. 'Nothing at all compared with you and Lana or Kieron and Ingrid.'

'Who?' said Kieron's mum, and both the boys were silenced.

I'd wanted to catch Paddy before his match with Charlie, but I was too late. They'd been on Court One in front of a surprisingly large audience, with several photographers making a nuisance of themselves. I caught Paddy's eye as I sat down, but he glowered at me. My God, he looked absolutely furious.

Down the other end, Charlie was a picture of concentration, despite the frivolous blond spikes on his head. No sense at all that he might be giving the match away. No sign either that his left knee was giving him any trouble.

But Paddy was playing a blinder. He was a fireball of energy – like Boris Becker used to be. He didn't miss anything. And he was hitting so hard, slamming shots at Charlie like bullets, as if he wanted to injure him. It was exciting stuff, and the spectators sensed it. Under-16 tennis wasn't usually this good.

Paddy took the first set almost before Charlie realised. The second set was going to be tougher. Charlie got into his stride, and he made good use of his height at the net. There was a game where Paddy couldn't get anything past him.

It was awful, I so much wanted Paddy to win. I sent thought signals to him, like I do when we play as partners. *Lob him. Lob him. Do an ace, now. Keep him running*. Maybe Charlie was simply too good for him. They only play best of three sets at this level. If Charlie got this set – well, anything could happen.

Charlie did take the second set after a tie-break. It was that close. Paddy wouldn't look at me as they sat down to rest between sets. I'd have to use telepathy again.

As everyone said, Paddy was incredibly fit. I happened to know he'd had a better night's sleep than Charlie, too (as long as he hadn't been tormented like I had). He just had to keep Charlie on the run, exhaust him, not give him a chance to win at the net, serve aces. The tension was hideous. Charlie was too good. No, Charlie *wasn't* too good. Give Paddy credit, I thought. At least think positive on his behalf.

Paddy had spotted that weak left knee. Again and again he made Charlie turn and run to the left. It was a cruel trick, maybe, but one that required a huge amount of skill of Paddy's part to make it come off. He made Charlie reach higher and higher at the net, forcing him to jump. Paddy's eyes were gimlet sharp, his forehead creased. It was as if he was fighting for his life.

Four–two. Paddy had broken Charlie's serve. In the next game the spin on Paddy's serve was so deceptive he managed to wrong-foot Charlie every time. I hardly dared to look, but I think the knee was beginning to play up under the punishment. Five–two. I had to leave, I couldn't bear the suspense.

Five minutes later, from the depth of the clubhouse I heard the cheer go up. Paddy had beaten Charlie, and I knew that Charlie had not willingly conceded a single point. Wow. What a performance!

I went out and watched the two of them shaking

hands with the umpire and coming off court in a blitz of camera flash. Charlie spotted me first. He gave me an exhausted grin. 'As I said,' he murmured as he passed, 'I expected the finalists to be better than me. No question, Paddy *won*, OK?'

I couldn't help it. I rushed up to Paddy and gave him a hug. But it was like hugging a splintery wooden post – with barbed wire on it.

I stepped back quickly. Was he angry with *me*? Was it sheer anger that had made him win?

Paddy and Charlie disappeared into the changing rooms. Robin and Lucy were suddenly at my elbow. 'Did you see that?' asked Robin. 'I've never seen Charlie totalled like that before, not even by one of the men. That was genius play.'

'Yup,' said Lucy. 'Respect for Paddy gone up by one hundred per cent. Not that I didn't respect him before. I should think you're quite proud of your partner, aren't you, Al?'

'He's ignoring me, Lucy. It's awful.'

'Paddy? Why?'

'I'm not sure. Something to do with last night.'

'Uh?' Lucy saw I needed to talk. 'Robin – I expect you want to go and commiserate with your old mate, don't you? Talk up the next match and so on?' Lucy gave him a piercing look.

'Oh, OK,' said Robin. 'I'll be off then.'

'Far-distant court,' said Lucy, taking me by the elbow. 'I think there are things I should know. I was a bit wrapped up in Robin last night. Seems like I didn't get the whole picture.'

We sat down and I told her about last night. After all,

she had something to do with it. 'Remember the challenge?'

I told her about Max playing along and teaching me how to do a stage kiss and then Charlie joining in.

'Ooh, so you made it up with Charlie did you? Great. So you *can* be a foursome with us. Not so sure about the bleached hair though.'

'I know. It was a perfectly nice colour before. It's quite cool though.'

'Didn't think you noticed these things.'

'Watch it.' It was nice talking to Lucy again. Megan had breezed in and out of my life like fresh air, but I've known Lucy for centuries. She knows the background. 'And no, Charlie and I won't be making a foursome with you and Robin. He doesn't take me seriously.'

'Unlike Paddy?'

'And what is that supposed to mean?'

'Oh come on Alex? Haven't you noticed the way Paddy looks at you these days?'

'With a face like thunder last time I saw him.'

'Has it never occurred to you that he might have feelings for you beyond being your tennis partner?'

'No.'

'And you can honestly say that you don't have *any* feelings for him outside the tennis court (you sad woman)?'

'Well—'

'Ha! You hesitated!'

'Well, I did kind of hope he'd turn up last night.'

'And he did.'

'Yeah, but he turned straight round and went home again.'

'Because he saw you canoodling with Charlie?'

'And with Max!'

'So that makes it better does it?' Lucy was laughing at me.

I protested. 'But I don't care about Max or Charlie! It was all only for this stupid romance thing anyway. I wish I'd never agreed to it. I've just made a complete and utter idiot of myself, and lost a good friend in the process!'

'You haven't lost Paddy. You've got to play a match with him this afternoon. Anyway, if he is angry, it can only be because he *likes* you, can't it?'

'You don't think – you don't think – that Paddy *likes* me, like that, do you?'

'Pea-brain! What do you think I've been trying to tell you *all* week?'

'Ohmygod! But that's awful! I mean – I never quite thought of that, until the Charlie kissing me thing, I suppose—'

'Make up your mind, would you? I know you don't *do* romance, don't think of boys "in that way" – you've told me nothing else. But I'm beginning to think the lady doth protest too much. You've been trailing blokes after you all week, and one in particular!'

'We're talking Paddy here? Tell me, because I'm getting confused.'

'YES!'

'Oh.'

I needed to be on my own. I told Lucy I didn't want to keep her from Robin any longer, and took a little walk into the car park. Only a few parents chatting on their mobiles or listening to the cricket there. Paddy, my friend and partner, was angry because he'd seen me apparently kissing Charlie. It only made sense if he had – feelings – for me. But he was my mate. How could I play tennis with him if I knew he felt like that about me?

I paced about. What would Megan say? She seemed to get to the quick of the matter before most people. Actually, Megan had said something last night – what was it? 'I think he's jealous' and 'something going on behind those gorgeous dark blue eyes.'

I thought about Paddy's eyes for a moment. They are a gorgeous colour – kind of navy-blue, and the giraffe lashes . . .

Oh dear. This didn't get any better.

I forced myself to think about something else. I wondered how the boys' doubles was going. Paddy (well, I *tried* to think about something else) and Richard were playing Tom Smart and a bloke called Toby; Neil and Raj were against Charlie and Robin. I suddenly felt all protective about our Club posse. You expect people with years of expensive coaching to do well, but we're a bit home-grown, if you know what I mean. I decided to track down Neil and Raj before their match began and tell them to play on Robin and to exploit Charlie's knee injury. I found them at the snack bar. 'Hi Al! How you doin'?' Raj was very cheery. He'd gone blond the night before too.

'Great! You two going to win then?'

'Of course,' said Neil.

'Of course,' said Raj.

'Well, maybe not,' said Neil.

'No. Probably not at all.'

'In fact we're almost certain to lose,' said Raj.

'Right boys. I've got news for you. You *are* going to win, and here's how.' I drew them into a corner and told them. 'You owe it to the Club, OK?'

'Yes ma'am!' said Neil, clicking his heels. Their match was called at that precise moment, so off they went, joshing each other and laughing.

Then Lucy appeared. 'So who are you going to watch?' she asked.

'Well I'm not watching Paddy.'

'That settles it then. Let's go and watch Robin.'

'And Neil and Raj. They're going to win, you know.'

'Oh yeah?'

The boys' match went on for ever, and I was glad. I wasn't looking forward to my next encounter with Paddy. What's more, it all served to tire Charlie out, and I wanted him to be dying of exhaustion by the time it came to our match. Neil and Raj put up a really good show. They kept up the pressure on Robin. Lucy didn't know who to support in the end. All three sets were close but Raj and Neil hung on in there to the last: 8–6, 6–8, 8–6. Lucy was thrilled for them, but she was even more thrilled to be able to comfort Robin. He and Charlie came over to us afterwards. 'Two defeats down,' Charlie said to me, 'and I'm knackered.'

'You're not supposed to let me know that,' I said.

'It's obvious, isn't it? And I think this great surgical bandage round my knee might be a bit of a giveaway.'

'Are you OK?'

'What do you care? Paddy's after my blood anyway, so I don't stand a chance. Man, he was ace this morning.

Think my coach ought to see him in action.' He turned his back on Robin. 'He's better than Robin.'

'Charlie! Ssh!'

'True.' He put his foot up on to a seat to ease his leg. 'Got to make him forgive me first. Could it be that Paddy is keener than we realised on a certain person not a million miles from here? Number one fan, in fact, of the club of which I'm a founder member?'

I blushed. 'I don't know, Charlie. I genuinely don't know.'

'Come on Charlie,' said Robin. 'A free drink awaits. We ought to go and claim it.'

'See you in a bit, Alex,' said Charlie. 'And just play on Louise OK? Leave my knee out of it. I might want to walk again one day.'

Paddy and Richard had lost. The mixed doubles semi-final couldn't be put off any longer. We were on court two, and quite a few parents had gathered to watch.

We filed onto the court. Paddy nodded at me. He didn't speak, just picked up a few balls ready to knock. Louise did her annoying hip-waggle down to the other end, ponytail swinging officiously as she herded Charlie into position.

'Paddy – please tell me what's wrong,' I said.

'Let's just get on with the match, shall we?'

'Play on Louise,' I said. 'Keep it away from Charlie at the net.'

'Do you think I don't know that?' he said. If what everyone implied was true, and he did like me, he certainly wasn't showing any signs of it now. He was right really, there was nothing for it but to get on with the match.

Louise fancied Charlie. Since Joel was already spoken for, she was determined to turn on the charm for Charlie. So she was showing off to him and playing incredibly well. Paddy didn't trust our usual empathy, but roared instructions at me all the time: 'Over there!' 'Yours!' 'Leave it!' 'Run, for Pete's sake!' And it didn't work. We tripped over each other the whole time. I lost confidence.

Louise and Charlie won the first set. Both boys seemed to have found a second wind. I suppose mixed doubles is a bit gentler for them. But I had to say something to Paddy.

'Please relax a bit, Paddy. We're great together usually – don't spoil it.'

And then he looked at me. A beautiful, raw, dark-blue gaze, piercing me to the heart.

It brought tears to my eyes. I put my hand on his arm. 'You got it wrong, Paddy. Trust me?' Our eyes locked for a few moments. I smiled. 'Let's get on with the match shall we?'

So we won. OK, maybe Charlie had to lose, but we were the better team. Louise got tired of showing off, Charlie's knee wasn't great, and the famous Dunbar–Gardner partnership came into its own.

Dad was there, clapping away with the best of them. 'Two Dunbars in the finals. *Ex*cellent result!'

Phil was with him. 'Well done, guys. You deserved to win that.'

'Get your gear together,' said Dad. 'Tonight something unprecedented is happening. Because the twins and Joel are out for the evening, the rest of us are going for a pizza.'

'What, Mum as well?'

'Yes, her idea. Not quite sure what's come over her, but I think we should take her up on it before she changes her mind, don't you?'

'See you tomorrow then,' said Paddy, with another of those looks.

So I left, without saying goodbye to Charlie or Robin, and with my 'relationship' with Paddy about as different as it could be from how it had been only three hours earlier. I felt all fluttery. At what precise moment does a friendship turn into a so-called 'relationship'?

Eleven

'You're very quiet Alex.'

'Sorry, Dad. A bit tired, that's all.'

'Too much fun last night,' said Phil.

'You're on dangerous ground, Phil,' I glared at him.

'Anyway, I'm very proud of you both,' said Dad. 'And everyone from the Club. I heard Paddy played well.'

'Paddy beat that Charlie guy,' said Phil. 'I only saw a bit of the match, but everyone was talking about it. And Charlie's as good as anyone in the under-18s.'

Please don't talk about Paddy.

'So why the pizza, Mum?'

'It seemed like a nice idea. You know, just to have a night off from cooking once in a while.'

'I'm all for it,' said Dad, giving Phil and me an isn't-this-great? look. It crossed my mind that we had no idea how Mum and Dad related to each other. They must have loved each other once. They were still together, weren't they?

'Maybe we should cook sometimes,' I said. 'You too, Dad. Rather than helping, perhaps we should give Mum more evenings off.'

'Ooh,' said Mum. 'I shouldn't know what to do with myself.'

'Watch EastEnders?' said Phil.

'Join a choir?' said Dad.

'Driving lessons?' I murmured.

FRIDAY

Know your partner's game as well as your own.

EVENT/S	VENUE	WEATHER CONDITIONS	PHYSICAL HEALTH
U-16 mixed	Mapledon	Sunny	Curse, bearable

OPPONENT
Louise Smart and Charlie.

TACTICS
Played ruthlessly on Louise.

RESULT
Won

EQUIPMENT
As before.

COMMENTS
I think I'm in love with Paddy.

TOMORROW'S MATCH
Mixed doubles v Phchang and partner.
Paddy also in the singles final against Tom Smart.

I went to bed as soon as we got back. Partly because of my bad night last night, but mostly to be on my own. I felt fine physically. As Megan had predicted, my first period turned out to be a one-day wonder and seemed to have fizzled out. I only had the next ten million years to look forward to. But it was as if my entire life had shifted. It wasn't only my body. It was Paddy. Mum as well.

As I lay there, I invented little scenarios for me and Paddy to star in. There was the one where our end-of-match handshake turned into a kiss in front of the cheering crowds. The one where we wandered off hand-in-hand to the woods by the car park. The one where we met at the beginning of the day and he told me that he'd been in love with me all summer.

In love? Was this me, Alex Dunbar, dreaming of love and romance? Things *had* changed! I found myself remembering little things about the way Paddy looked. He was certainly fit. Not tall, but taller than me, just. Lightish brown hair, slightly sun-streaked. Ordinary nose, possibly on the blobby side. Full lips. Smily lips. Nice teeth (though I'd spare him any comments). Quite a fair skin. Possibly a freckle or two. And dark blue eyes with black curling lashes.

And the kindest, most steadfast, cheerful nature. Until yesterday of course, though perhaps a little anger in the right places was no bad thing. And he mostly took it out on the tennis ball. In fact, he was so gorgeous, why hadn't I noticed before? And if he was so gorgeous, probably there were queues of far more suitable girls just waiting to grab him for themselves.

PANIC!

Calm down, Alex, and go to sleep. I did.

Saturday morning. Finals Day – the big one. Perfect Finals Day weather, too. Late summer sunshine. For the first time in the tournament I had the confidence to wear tennis whites without covering them up with a dark tracksuit. About time I showed off my brown legs, anyway. Phil and I were both keyed up as we drove in with Kieron, though possibly for different reasons. Phil was worried about the tennis. I wasn't.

Paddy was nowhere to be seen. His match wasn't until two p.m. and our mixed doubles was much later in the afternoon. Phil and Kieron had to go off and play almost immediately so I was left to wander round on my own. Tom and Louise Smart were both singles *and* doubles finalists, so the Smarts were there in force, including the grandparents, all sporting a wide range of fashionable sunglasses, Scarlett included. Louise was making her presence felt, big time, swanning about as if she was champion already. I decided to go and watch the boys (Tom Smart and Toby versus Neil and Raj) rather than the girls (Louise Smart and Claire versus Alicia and Connie). Louise with her silly walk and bouncing pony-tail is too annoying. I needed someone to talk to and I was missing Lucy and Robin and Charlie already. They were all at the Prestige Gold Cup of course. Dad, Mum and the twins would arrive as soon as they'd dropped Joel off there.

I sat on the end of a row to watch. The boys were having a niggly sort of match. No one seemed to be winning or losing. I went into a daydream about Paddy.

I was dying to see him but dreading it at the same time. What if *I'd* got it all wrong? What if I was just imagining things? I was miles away when Paddy came and sat beside me. We were both in shorts and I suddenly felt embarrassed by the proximity of our bare legs.

'Who's winning?' asked Paddy (very romantic).

'Tom and Toby, just.' (Equally so.)

'Oh.'

'When's your match?' I asked, as if I didn't know.

'Two o'clock. Assuming this one's over.'

We both watched in silence as Tom served four aces in a row, followed by Neil serving four double faults.

'I'm too nervous to watch this,' said Paddy. 'See you later.' And he was gone before I could ask anything important, or even catch his eye. As he left, there was a roar of applause from the next court. It didn't seem fair on the boys to disturb them further by going to find out who had won the girls' doubles, but there was no need, because the entire Smart clan, looking sombre, filed into the back row to watch Tom and Toby cranking out a narrow win. The long faces meant that the title had been won by Alicia and Connie and that Louise had even more to play for in her singles against Alicia.

I saw my family arriving in force but they turned off to watch Phil and Kieron. It was time for the junior singles finals. The boys' and the girls' matches were on adjacent courts, so it was possible to keep an eye on both. The Smarts took up most of the standing space between the courts. There was no escaping the fact that they had a finalist in each. As the four players filed through a single gate I saw Louise in animated conversation with Paddy – she obviously had something exciting to tell him, because he was listening, despite his pre-match psyching up routine (that I would never dream of interrupting). Tom was completely relaxed. He looked fresh as a daisy. Poor Paddy.

My emotions during that game went through more highs and lows than I have ever experienced in my life. They had become as untrustworthy as my body! I was fearful for Paddy. I was proud of him. I wanted him to win so badly it hurt. He wasn't driven by anger like he was against Charlie, but then Tom Smart wasn't as good as Charlie, and he had just played a match even if it hadn't been very strenuous. While I was sitting there two men with Australian accents plonked themselves down next to me. 'Which fellow is it?' one asked the other.

'That one. Must be. Charlie didn't say anything about bleached hair.'

'Beaut backhand. Look at that.'

'He's fast.'

'You can say that again.'

They were talking about Paddy, but they were distracting him. He glanced up in our direction. 'Ssh!' I said to the two men.

'Apologies,' whispered the designer-stubble one. 'Good girl. You stick by your young fella. He's going places, I'd put money on it.'

They wrote a few things down and then slipped away. I felt all excited. Paddy was going to be a tennis star! *But if he's a tennis star he won't be interested in me any more.* I was up and down like a yoyo. I just wanted the match to be over. Then again, I wanted it to go on for ever.

Paddy beat Tom in straight sets! Yippee! I ran over to congratulate him, but the two boys were surrounded by their families and other people too. To make matters worse, Louise won her match a few minutes later so the crowd of Smarts and others got bigger. Then, in front of my eyes, Louise and Paddy were pushed back on to the court by a group of photographers who wanted pictures of the two new junior champions. They were making them do all these ridiculous poses together. It was nauseating. And there was no Charlie to distract Louise either.

I gave up in disgust and went to find some Dunbars, not hard when someone as large as Mum is involved. They'd moved on to the under-18 boys' singles. For once the twins were totally rapt – I've never seen them sitting so still. Kieron was with them. 'Not a patch on Paddy and Charlie yesterday,' he whispered. 'Who won over there?'

'Paddy did and so did Louise.'

'Oh boy. Did he now?' Kieron craned his neck to see the photographers' antics. 'Paddy might not know it, but he is about to join the Smart set. "Call-me-Janice" loves winners – shame the loser had to be Tom.'

'Paddy loathes the Smart scene.'

'He'll have a battle on his hands then.'

I felt comfortable with Kieron and my lot. I decided to stay there until our mixed doubles was called. In between sets I heard a familiar voice. It was Megan, with a boy who looked about the same age as Jack and Sam. 'Hi guys,' she said in a stage whisper. They sat down. 'This is David. You have to keep your mouth shut when they're playing, David, or they shoot you.'

'It's OK, I know,' said David. 'Stop being embarrassing.'

Mum and Megan exchanged sympathetic looks.

Megan turned to me. 'This is going to go on for a while, isn't it? Do you want to wander about, fill me in on the gossip? David will be OK with your folks, won't he?'

'Yes, yes and yes.'

We slipped away. 'OK,' she said. 'Spill the beans. What's going on with you and Paddy?'

'Nothing!'

'I don't believe you!' She was using that sing-song voice again. 'A guy doesn't walk away in disgust from a friend who happens to be kissing two other guys simultaneously unless he fancies her.'

'I wasn't really kissing them.'

'That's how it looked to me. And to Paddy as well, I presume.'

'Well, I suppose it's not entirely true to say that *nothing* is going on. It's just that I'm not sure what.' We had arrived at the far-distant court with the table. 'Yesterday he wouldn't look at me and seemed to be incredibly angry.'

'Jealous, I told you so.'

'And his match against Charlie was completely amazing. He looked as though he was trying to kill him.'

'As I said. Jealous.'

'Then we had to play together and he was completely horrible to me at first.'

'Jealous.'

'Until – I just asked him to stop it. I told him he'd got it wrong and that he should trust me.'

'Jealous as a parrot.'

'Will you stop staying that! Anyway, it's sick as a parrot.'

'Same thing.'

I hit her, and continued. 'I didn't actually say *what* he'd got wrong, or *how* he should trust me.'

'And you think he doesn't know?'

'From the way he *looked* at me, I think he did. But I haven't spoken to him since then – apart from "nice shot" and "leave it" and that sort of thing. Our family went out for a pizza and he'd gone to bed when I phoned afterwards and today he wouldn't look me in the eye again when we saw each other.

'Ah. Was it a gooey look – yesterday?'

'I suppose it was.'

'Did it make your legs go all funny?'

'I suppose it did. Ooh, I don't know what to do, Megan. I've never had feelings like this before. When I first met you, all of three days ago, I was still one of the lads. And look at me now!'

She raised her eyebrows and gave me a knowing smirk.

'Enough of that. This is quite different. But I still need help!'

'Can't help. You've got your match with him soon. See how that goes. I shall be observing both your expressions very closely.'

'I'm feeling all nervous now,' I looked at my watch. 'It's four-fifteen. We'll have to start soon. The prize-giving's at six.'

Bang on cue: 'Under-16 Mixed Doubles finalists please. Patrick Gardner and Miss Alexandra Dunbar. Lee Barclay and Miss Philippa Chang. (Full names for finalists.) Court Three in five minutes please.'

'I'll come with you as far as the others. I'd better see that David's behaving himself.'

'Thanks. I can't believe how scared I feel.'

When Megan left me to go to Court Three on my own I felt like a lamb going to the slaughter. It was silly, because I'd beaten Phchang in the singles, and whoever Lee Barclay was he couldn't be as good as Paddy – this year's champion. (That was so cool!) Lee and Phchang were already knocking up. The umpire was up on her seat. We even had a couple of ballboys (girls). Paddy made a bit of a hero's entrance, the crowd parting and pointing at the new champion. He didn't look nervous at all. He came over to me with a wide Paddy grin.

'OK? This one's easy,' he said.

'Well done for winning – I couldn't get to you afterwards. Media frenzy.'

'We might be interviewed on local TV later!'

'Wow!' I'd tell him about Charlie's Australians later. He was so happy, his eyes were sparkling and his step was even more springy than usual. Just the sight of him made me feel weird and trembly.

We started our knock-up. I seemed to trip over my own feet a bit, but that's par for the course when you start completely cold. I should have been hitting against the practice wall rather than chatting with Megan. Paddy was flying, though, so my little errors didn't really show. Until, that is, we started playing. Paddy won his service game – no worries. Lee didn't quite get into the swing of his. But then I completely bodged all mine. Double fault after double fault. 'Never mind,' said Paddy. 'We can afford to lose one game.'

But I'd lost it. Not just the game – *it*. My telepathy had gone, for a start. I no longer had a clue what Paddy was going to do next. We kept bumping into each other, and when we did, well, the physical contact turned me even more to jelly.

'I'm so sorry,' I said to Paddy when the other two won the first set. 'I don't know what's come over me.' And then when he turned his sympathetic blue eyes on me I simply melted away.

He smiled a very small and secret smile. 'It's what I was afraid of at the beginning of the week,' he said almost to himself. And then, louder. 'Never mind! Twelve more games and the match is ours!'

In fact, eight more games and the match was theirs. The only ones we won were Paddy's service games. It was so humiliating. The applause from those who'd bothered to stay on was half-hearted.

'You were useless, Al!' said Jack as the family crowded round me afterwards.

'Paddy was brilliant! He should have a better partner,' said Sam.

'Thanks, boys, for your support,' I said.

'Keep quiet you two,' said Mum severely. *Mum?* 'You don't know what it's like out there for the big match.'

'And I suppose you do?' said Jack cheekily.

'As a matter of fact she does,' said Dad, weighing in.

'On this very court as a matter of fact,' said Mum, without sighing. My mouth was hanging open. 'With your dad. Wasn't it, dear?'

'How come we never knew this?' Phil was staggered too.

'No secret,' said Dad. 'Just a hideously long time ago. Never mind, Alex. You've done very well to be a finalist. I'm proud of you. And Paddy'll be up there getting his cup along with Phil. Our little club does it again!'

There were one or two matches still finishing off but the organisers were setting up the prize-giving on Court One. The cups and salvers and teaspoons (that's what I'd get) lay in shining array on the white-clothed trestle table. The local mayor was there, chain and all, along with the Mapledon Club worthies. I left my family to join the other finalists. As I passed Megan she said, 'Bad luck for losing. Think you might be a winner in other ways though. I saw the looks he gave you. His game was affected too, you know!'

'We still haven't talked.'

'Your chance will come. I'd better get out of the way before I'm mown down by gentlemen of the press. Go on. Go and claim Paddy before Louise eats him.'

I pushed through the crowd. Once we were all on court the proceedings began. Lots of speeches about talented youngsters and thanks to the ladies who provided the teas, etc. First the under-16s: Louise and Paddy (Mr Popular – the cheer for him was enormous); Alicia and Connie; Tom and Toby, Phchang and Lee. They all stood in a row with their cups and platters. Then the runners-up: Alicia went up again; so did Tom; Louise again and Claire; Raj and Neil; and then me and Paddy (still hugging his cup – up went the cheer again). He turned to me with a smile and lifted my arm in a sort of wave to the onlookers. The photographers went wild. Flash. Flash. Flash.

Then we all stood back and the under-18s (including Phil and Kieron) went through the same rigmarole. I was squashed against Paddy. He kept beaming at me, but this wasn't the time to have a meaningful conversation. I hoped that would come later. As we made our way off the court the two Australians were waiting for Paddy.

They asked to be introduced to his parents and I lost him. Worse still, when he reappeared, Louise waggled up to him, saying that the four singles champions were wanted down at the local TV studio. Her parents were going to give them a lift. I saw Ethlie running after them, still trying to be part of the action.

So there I was. All hyped up and nowhere to go. Megan and David had to catch the bus home. Dad was ready to take us. The week was over. It was all over. Carrying my tennis bag and my teaspoon I followed the others to the car.

Twelve

'Mum, it's them. Come and watch.'

Slip-slop, sigh. 'I'm too busy with the supper. Phil was meant to be helping and now they've all gone off with your father to get Joel.'

'Come on Mum. Quick. It'll only last a second. I'll help you when it's over.'

Slip-slop, floomph (Mum sitting on the sofa). 'Oh, there's you and Paddy!'

It was. One of the cameras must have been a camcorder. I wished I'd set the video. There for all the world to see was Paddy smiling and me blushing as he raised our arms in front of the Mayor. Cut to the studio.

Oh great. There was Louise, sparkling vivaciously as she sat knee-to-knee with Paddy. The interviewer kept on about these players of the future, names to watch etc. He asked Paddy if the final had actually been his hardest match of the tournament. 'Definitely not,' said Paddy. His semi-final had been hardest.

Then Louise interrupted and said that her final had been her toughest, and the two under-18s were brought into the discussion before we were suddenly on to the next item about a traffic-calming scheme.

'The local paper was the pinnacle of news coverage in my time,' said Mum. 'TV news seems very grand.'

'Mum, how come you've never talked about this before? I knew that you'd played at some point, but not that you actually played with Dad at Mapledon.'

'Well,' said Mum. 'Look at me. As you can see, my tennis playing days are long gone.'

'Mum, nobody has to be – overweight – these days. They're always telling us that in PSE at school.'

Mum stood up abruptly (for her). She sighed again. 'Well, madam. You'll find out one day just how hard it is to raise a family and be all things to all people.'

'But Mum—' She was off, slip-slopping into the kitchen to bang things about. I followed her. 'Mum, if I stay and help, will you carry on talking to me, without "madam-ing" me. I am your daughter, you know.'

'All right, all right.'

'Could it be that you're – depressed? They tell us about that at school as well. Not to mention on Rikki Lake and Jerry Springer.'

'Maybe.'

'Have you been to a doctor?'

'Alex! That's enough now.'

I felt dogged. 'I don't see why I shouldn't ask. It was

something Megan said, Mum. She said, "at least you've got a mother". Which is true. And Megan hasn't. But I thought – don't get me wrong, Mum – I thought, well, I do have a Mum but she doesn't seem all that happy to have me. I always thought you picked on me because you were – well – a grumpy personality. But if you *are* depressed, and you could get undepressed, well, that would be great.'

'If only it was that simple. Now I really must get on.'

'Mum! You're being defeatist before you've even begun. You know what Dad says about that.'

'No, what does he say?'

'Well, you can still win even when you're six–love five–love down, and stuff. He's got lots of things like that.'

The boys crashed in at that point: Dad, Phil, Joel, Jack, Sam. All demanding food. All talking about the day's sport. Noisy. Perhaps I know why Mum's overwhelmed. We had supper. I tried to tell them about being on the news, but they didn't hear. Joel, on a high from winning his matches, picked a quarrel with Jack. Sam joined in. Phil slammed out. Dad tried to stay cheerful.

'I'm going upstairs,' I said.

'It's barely nine o'clock,' said Dad.

'I didn't say I was going to bed. Just to my room. I'm tired.'

Just then there was a shout from the front room. 'I'm on the telly!' It was Phil. Everyone rushed in. 'Ooh look! There's Alex and Paddy.' There we were again. I so much wanted to see Paddy, to talk to him. To—

'Yuk! They're holding hands.'

'Is Paddy your boyfriend, Alex? Does he snog you?'

I saw red. 'SHUT UP!' I screamed. 'LEAVE ME ALONE!'

'Yes, leave the poor girl alone,' said Mum sternly as I ran from the room.

As I sat on my bed sobbing, I imagined Paddy with Louise and the Smarts. I could practically hear Louise chatting him up. After all, I'd heard her smarming round Joel and Charlie. They all love winners in that family. What if they'd asked him back afterwards? The phone rang. I shot out of my room to grab the cordless one on the landing. It was Lucy.

'Hang on while I take it into my room.'

'I just saw you and Paddy on the telly. Sorry you didn't win the mixed, but isn't it great about Paddy? I had a brilliant time with Robin and Charlie at the Cup. Wish I was still with them. After all, it is Saturday night. How did your day go? And I don't mean the tennis.'

'We still haven't talked, Lucy. It's crazy. Paddy kept being whisked off. I last saw him disappearing in the Smarts' car on the way to the TV studio with Louise all over him.'

'He was smiling very fondly at you on the telly. You were holding hands!'

'No we weren't! He was just making me wave. Lucy, do you think I should ring him? I don't know what I'd say, but—'

'Why not? Nothing to lose.'

'I'll die if they say he's still at the Smarts. Or if he wonders why I've rung.'

'Go on. Ring him now and ring me back. I order you to.'

I dialled Paddy's number and put the phone straight down. But Lucy would be waiting. I dialled again. Mrs Gardner answered. 'Hallo? Could I speak to Paddy please?'

'He's not here, I'm afraid. Those Smart people have taken him out for a meal. I wish he was here. There's an Australian coach who keeps ringing and I don't know when Paddy will be back.'

'Perhaps you could ring the Smarts on their mobile?'

'I wouldn't know the number – do you?'

'They might give it in their answerphone message.'

'That's a very good idea. I'll give it a try. And shall I tell Paddy you rang?'

'Yes, OK. Tell him – tell him to meet Alex up at the Club tomorrow morning – nine o'clock, please.'

'I will, Alex.'

'Lucy? He's only out to dinner with the Smarts! But I was brave. I left a message for him to meet me at nine o'clock tomorrow morning.'

'That's a very romantic hour!'

'It's all I could think of. Twelve hours from now.'

'Aren't you coming to the Cup tomorrow? Robin and Charlie get to play Joel.'

'Did Charlie tell you he'd sent his coach to talent scout? Paddy's mum says they've been ringing already.'

'Shows that Charlie's a nice guy. Not everyone would be so generous.'

'Something to do with his confidence. And I'll tell you something else about Charlie.'

'Something I don't know?'

'He's a damn fine kisser!'

'Alex! You *have* changed!'

'I was just thinking about it. I'm kind of glad he gave me a bit of practice. Now I'll know what to do with Paddy when I get him on his own.'

'Wonders will never cease, Alex Dunbar!'

'You were the one who tried to convince me that it might be fun.'

'And is it?'

'We'll see, won't we?'

SATURDAY

You can cover the whole range of emotions in a game of tennis, from anger and frustration to joy and to calm.

EVENT/S	VENUE	WEATHER CONDITIONS	PHYSICAL HEALTH
U-16 mixed	Mapledon	Sunny	Great (Emotional health, variable)

OPPONENT
Phchang and partner.

TACTICS
None (tactics beyond me).

RESULT
Lost

EQUIPMENT
Bat and ball of course.

COMMENTS
I'm completely in love with Paddy.
I hate Louise Smart.

TOMORROW'S MATCH
Ha-ha! Me and Paddy 9 a.m.

'Just off to the club!' I took my racquet. This wasn't abnormal behaviour in our family.

'Hi!' Paddy was already there, face lit up, but nervous.

'How was last night?'

'My Smart night out? OK. It was a nice meal. "Call-me-Janice" and Louise talked non-stop. They want me to join Highcliffe tennis club.'

'Paddy! You won't will you?'

'Course not.'

'So what about the Aussie tennis coach? Has he rung again?'

'Not yet. It's quite cool, isn't it?' He looked me in the eye. 'So why did you want to meet me up here?'

'I – just wanted to talk. Sort a few things out.'

'Like what?' He was smiling at me.

'Well, I'm sorry I let you down yesterday.'

'That's OK.'

'Paddy!' He was being infuriating. 'You're really making me work, aren't you?'

'Yup.'

'OK. I wanted to go back to Friday, when I told you you'd got it wrong.'

'Uh-huh.'

'Grrrr! OK then. Thursday night. I'm not going to beat about the bush any more, so serves you right if I embarrass you.'

'I'm listening.'

'Thursday night. At the Smarts. You arrive. And I appear to be kissing Max and Charlie. The truth is extremely silly, but you'll have to believe me. I was on a dare if you like – more a promise – with some friends from school, to have a romance during the tournament.'

'Ironic,' said Paddy.

'As you well know, I have no experience in these matters at all.'

'No good at reading the signs?'

'No.' I narrowed my eyes at him. *What did that mean?* 'Time was running out, so in desperation I asked Max to *pretend* to have a romance with me. And you know what Max is like – he was up for it. And he was *pretending* to kiss me, you know, with his hand over his mouth, when Charlie came along and thought it was some sort of game he could join in and kissed me – for a laugh.'

'I knew all along that Charlie fancied you.'

'Not really, Paddy. It was just a laugh, honestly. And I didn't start it, OK?'

'I could have killed Charlie.'

'Now you have to tell me why.'

'At the risk of embarrassing you? OK, here goes.' He spoke without looking at me. 'I sort of fancied my own chances with you. But you never seemed to notice me, apart from as a partner. So I thought perhaps it would be better if we weren't partners for a bit.'

'I just thought you'd gone off me.'

'Nah.' He managed a quick grin at me then. 'I also thought I might not play so well if I was concentrating more on the girl next to me than on the ball.'

'Precisely what happened to me yesterday.'

'I know!' he said, and laughed delightedly.

I thumped him. We were sitting on a bank by one of the tennis courts at the Club. A couple of extremely old people were playing on the farthest court. No one else was around. Paddy retaliated by throwing a handful of grass at me. I got up and ran round the back of the pavilion. Paddy, as I've often said, is fantastically fit, so it didn't take him long to catch up with me. He caught my wrists and leant towards me. He was still smiling but his dark blue eyes were looking into mine intently. I held his gaze for a few seconds before letting my eyelids close. His lips were incredibly soft and the way he held my face was just so tender. Of all the kisses I have had (three now) it was the sweetest.

We stood apart and looked at each other shyly.

'It's been a funny week,' I said, as we walked back to sit on our bank. Behind the pavilion is fairly unsavoury.

'For me too,' said Paddy. 'I was so angry on Thursday night and Friday morning. Looking back, I suppose that's why I beat Charlie. I never would have otherwise.'

'Never mind, the fact is, you did. You do know it was Charlie who put the talent scouts on to you, don't you?'

'Do you mean I have to thank the guy?'

'Apologise even.'

'Never!' He looked at me seriously again. 'Hey, I never thought it would turn out like this.'

'Me neither. It's good though. Now I have a romance to report back on.'

'You didn't just – this isn't just a dare, is it?'

He looked so panic-stricken I had to laugh. 'No. If it was a dare I would have put my hand over my mouth.'

'I'm glad you didn't.'

Our little rendezvous was soon brought to a halt by the club members arriving for their Sunday morning session. That was when Paddy let on that he'd agreed to partner his dad.

'So I just have to make myself scarce now, do I?'

'Unless you want to stay and watch.'

'I don't know what I want to do now. I feel all—'

'Churned up? So do I! When can we get together again?'

'It's never been difficult. We've always had an excuse. Ring me this afternoon. I might have been dragged off to watch the Cup, but keep ringing, OK?'

'Try and stop me.'

I walked home, almost danced home, taking the route I knew my dad wouldn't use. I was greeted by various club members on the way, cheery middle-aged men and women. They know me, even if I don't know them. They made me think.

When I got in, Joel had gone to the Cup, but the other boys were slobbing about in their various ways and Mum was slip-slopping and sighing her way round after them. My warm and generous mood was still with me.

'Do you want a cup of coffee, Mum?'

'What, dear?'

'Would you like to sit down and have me make you a cup of coffee?'

'Well, I don't know—'

'Sit!'

Who could refuse? I made some instant coffee for her and some instant hot chocolate for me and sat at the kitchen table with her. I'd had an idea. 'Mum?'

She looked at me warily. 'What is it now?'

'I want you to start playing tennis again.'

'That's all very well for you to—'

'I know you used to be good.'

'I don't think—'

'I'll play with you. We can go up to the Club when there's no one there. When I come home after school next term – no one goes up then. Please, Mum?'

'Why all this—'

'Because I know you'll enjoy it. And then when you've got your confidence back you can go and play on Sunday mornings with Dad. You ought to be up there with him.'

'Well, it's a nice thought, dear.'

'It's more than that, Mum. Just say you'll give it a try. Use one of the twins' racquets. Wear my spare trainers. No excuses.'

'All right. Maybe.'

Then Phil came in. 'What's for lunch, Mum? Are we going to eat before we go and watch Joel?'

'Oh dear, I'd better get a move on,' she said. 'We don't want to miss Joel, do we?'

Serve him right if we did, I thought. I went upstairs to my room.

I lay back on my bed. Happiness kept bubbling up. He kissed me! Paddy likes me! He's liked me all along! I guess I've got a boyfriend – I've had a holiday romance, even. More than a holiday romance, I hope. I don't have to say goodbye to Paddy like I would have had to to Charlie.

Charlie. He was kind of the catalyst in all this. The founder member of the Alex Dunbar fan club. Actually I did want to say goodbye to him, and thank him on Paddy's behalf. I decided to go along to the Cup with the others. It would be nice to see Lucy. And it would spare me the agony of waiting for the phone to ring.

Joel and his partner were losing to Charlie and Robin.

Joel is a bad loser. Unlike Paddy, he hadn't noticed Charlie's dodgy knee. Joel plays lovely shots, but he's frankly too selfish to notice things about other people, even to take advantage of their weak points. I looked round the spectators for Lucy. Claire was there below us, supporting Joel of course, and she had Louise with her. Tee-hee. I wondered how Louise would feel if she knew that Paddy and I were – whatever we were. Wretched girl. She'd better keep her hands off him from now on. And then I spotted Lucy over the other side. I decided to make my way over when the players changed ends. I had lots to tell Lucy.

'Robin said he'd come and find me here,' said Lucy. 'It's a good place to see people. I just saw Chris Green.'

'Who's he?'

'Tennis heart-throb. He is gorgeous. Louise Smart has the hots for him.'

'Louise has the hots for everyone. Joel, Charlie. It was Paddy last night.'

'I knew it wouldn't be long before you mentioned his name. OK, so what's the deal?'

'We—' I grinned.

'Thank goodness for that!' she said.

'Thank goodness for what?' said Charlie as he and Robin joined us.

'Alex and Paddy finally got it on.'

'Lucy!'

'Thank goodness for that,' said Charlie. 'Lucky bloke.' I looked at him questioningly. 'Can't deny I'm jealous,' he said. 'Snappy tennis player too.'

'He's really grateful about the coaching offer.'

'Glad to be of service,' said Charlie. 'Keep in touch won't you, Miss A. Dunbar? I might need some humour to lighten my life at school next term. Robin won't be much use.' Robin and Lucy were starting to say goodbye already, in an interactive hands-on sort of way.

'Of course, if you give me the address. Thanks, Charlie. For more than you realise.'

'As I said, glad to be of service.'

Joel appeared – unexpectedly as far as I was concerned.

'Hi guys. We're off, Al. Coming?'

'OK.' I unglued Robin from Lucy so I could give him a hug. 'Bye, Robin.'

'Maybe we'll visit you both at half-term?' he said.

Then Charlie. 'See ya,' said Charlie, '–before half-term I hope,' and I gave him a hug too. 'Easy does it,' he protested. 'I'm not Paddy!' And we were off.

'Bye!' Joel called after them. And, 'Bye, Chris, see ya next year!' He waved at someone in the distance.

'Who is this famous Chris Green?' I asked, intrigued now. 'I never manage to catch sight of him. Was he around last year? Dark curly hair?'

'That's the one. Do you remember him?'–

'Only just. I vaguely remember thinking he looked nice.'

'Well, now he happens to be the coolest guy and an ace tennis player. Comes from the Midlands somewhere. Maybe I'd better keep you away from him – with your reputation!'

'Joel!' I hit him.

'Well – last year, gangly tomboy sister – Alex, is that a

boy or a girl? This year – Kieron, Charlie, Paddy and I don't know who else!'

'No one else! Anyway – only keeping up with my brother.'

He laughed. And *that* was the first jokey conversation I have had with Joel since we used to play with make-up.

The day stayed good. As we came in the door, the phone was ringing. I rushed to pick it up, hoping it would be Paddy. It wasn't – it was Megan.

'Megan! I've got so much to tell you.' I burst out, but as I started running out of steam (about half an hour later), she said, 'Actually it was your mum I wanted to speak to. At least, I was going to put her on to my dad.'

'Mum?' I said, shocked. 'Mum, it's Megan's dad. For you.'

The others dispersed around the house, but I couldn't go too far away. I hung around the bottom of the stairs. Why on earth should my mother want to speak to Megan's father?

'Thanks,' I heard her say. 'Wednesday morning ten-thirty it is. You'll pick me up. Look forward to seeing you.'

Curiosity got the better of me. 'So what was all that about, Mum? What's Megan's dad got that my dad hasn't?'

'A driving instructor's qualification?'

I practically fainted. But then the phone rang again, and it was Paddy.

SUNDAY

Love tennis, love life.

EVENT/S	VENUE	WEATHER CONDITIONS	PHYSICAL HEALTH
Romantic encounter	The Club	Great	Great

OPPONENT
Paddy

TACTICS
Honesty

RESULT
Result!

EQUIPMENT
Heart

COMMENTS
Game, set and love match.

TOMORROW'S MATCH
Yay! And for ever!

Epilogue

I used to accuse Joel of being so self-obsessed that he never noticed what anyone else was thinking or doing, but now I think that I've been a bit like that too. It isn't all just about 'boys' and fancying them, is it? In fact I always had that empathy with Paddy, but I've noticed so much more about other people in this last week – it's quite spooky. Not that I now love all my fellow men and women or anything holy like that. I still think Ethlie's a pain in the butt, and I don't want to even try and understand how someone like Louise Smart ticks. It was Megan, I suppose. And having a glimpse of Mum and Dad as real people. I don't forgive my brothers for bullying and taunting me – Joel's old enough to know better. But the twins aren't. They need someone to tell them when they're out of order. That's all. I shouldn't let them get away with it.

And my family isn't that bad. I'd rather be a Dunbar than a Smart any day!

Paddy and I are having a brilliant time. We go to the Club a lot, because that's the easiest place to meet. It's not a going-out-on-the-town sort of relationship, and neither of us quite wants to take the other home. Yet.

I did think it might be possible to have the sleepover at our house (now there's a first), but Zoe said we should go to hers – she does have a lot more room and only one younger brother. I let on to her that I'd managed a romance, but we agreed to save the details until the sleepover even though I was itching to share it with her – of all people. I still couldn't believe I had something to report! Holly's back too, but we keep missing each other. The others are all in for such a surprise!

Zoe practically has the whole basement to herself in their house, and the food is real fabbo help-yourself-to-anything-in-the-freezer stuff. Her mum is not fat. Could there be some connection?

I'd been shopping in the last few days and bought some baggy trousers and little top like the one Megan lent me. I scraped my hair up too. Didn't want my friends thinking I was exactly the same unsophisticated Alex they knew and loved.

'Hey!' said Zoe. 'A new-look Alex, then?'

'Oh, not so different. You're used to me in baggy trousers.'

'Yeah, but I've never seen the belly button before.'

'That's because it's new.'

Zoe gave me a hug. 'Oooh! Can't wait!' she squealed, just as the other two arrived. There was lots more squealing and hugging. We loaded up with food and went down into Zoe's room. 'OK, who's going first?' said Zoe. We decided to go in alphabetical order, perfect when you have an A and a Z. I felt as though I was making a speech at an award ceremony and that I ought to thank everyone who'd made my romance possible, but the others screamed at me to stop messing around and get on with it. So I did. I told them about Kieron and Charlie and Paddy (of course), but also about Megan and Mum and the fact that I now had as good an excuse for being grumpy once a month as they had.

Holly was next. Holly's so pretty that if something went wrong with one guy I'm sure there'd always be another there to take his place, though I couldn't quite work out what order things were happening in while she was staying at her boyfriend's stately home. She was beating her breast about some girl who sounded like a waste of space to me and I found myself daydreaming about Paddy and not listening – until the name Chris Green popped up. I tuned in, rapidly. 'Not the Chris Green who was playing in the Cup in Hertfordshire?' And it seems that it was! Oh well, no point at all in Joel introducing me if Holly's in the picture. I know my place in the pecking order.

Josie seems to have made a beeline for her best friend's boyfriend, which of course didn't go down well with the best friend, and it was all our fault for forcing her to have a romance when she was wearing a brace. Still, matters improved enormously *later on, apparently. It must be fun seeing the same people on holiday every year. Not unlike Mapledon I suppose.*

Zoe, after being frivolous in Tuscany earlier on, worked incredibly hard at the Community Theatre Project and met loads of really grown-up people. I sometimes wonder how she tolerates me as a friend when each time I begin catching up with her she leaps on ahead. I feel she's at least six years older than me. But the fact is, she does.

And so do the others, jokes and all. So does Paddy. And, do you know? I can't think of a single funny thing to say about it.

Also in the *GIRLS LIKE YOU SERIES:*

Sophie

Blonde, drop-dead beautiful Sophie is used to getting her own way, and not worrying about the broken hearts she leaves behind. She's determined that a family camping holiday in France is not going to cramp her style. What's more she knows exactly who she wants . . . but does he feel the same way about her?

Hannah

Hannah is the clever one, and hard to please – but she's really shy too. She doesn't fancy her chances on a summer music course – so she decides that the boys are just not worth bothering about . . . not any of them . . . or are they?

Charlotte

Shy, dreamy Charlotte has been going to the Lake District every year for as long as she can remember and she's loved Josh from afar for as long. But this year she's going without her older sister. It might be the chance she's been waiting for. What if Josh notices her – just because she's four years younger than him – it doesn't mean all her dreams won't come true – does it?

Maddy

Finding romance has never been a problem for Maddy – she's always been a beauty and dramatic with it. So she can't wait for her exotic holiday in Barbados with Dad – it's going to be brilliant, and so different from life at home with impoverished Mum. The stage is set – but is romance all that lies in store for Maddy?

Holly

Holly is already in love – with Jonty, the boy she met in Barbados last year. Now she's on her way to stay with them at the family's country estate – complete with tennis courts and polo ponies – it sounds like a dream but will it turn out to be a nightmare?

Josie

Sun, sea and sand: a perfect setting for a holiday romance and Josie's off to a Cornish beach to find one. She's been spending her summers there since – well . . . forever, and this year she's determined to be Queen of the Scene in the popularity stakes, even if it means trying to pull her best friend's boyfriend! It's bound to end in tears for one of them – but who?

Zoe

The last thing smart, beautiful Zoe wanted to spend the last precious days of her summer holiday doing was taking her little brother to the local Community Theatre Project. But waiting in the wings is the mysterious, exciting, unpredictable Lennie and Zoe is swept off her feet by him and his passion for the Project. If only he could burn with the samc passion for her. Zoe decides to make it happen – but the results aren't quite what she expected!